A SUMMER FOLLY

Philippa Southcott was a very ambitious musician. When she gave a recital on her harp in the village church she met tall, dark-haired Alex Penfold, who had recently inherited the local Manor House, and couldn't get him out of her mind. Philippa didn't want anything or anyone to interfere with her career, least of all a man as disturbing as Alex, but keeping him at a distance turned out to be no easy matter!

*Books by Peggy Loosemore Jones
in the Linford Romance Library:*

MOON OVER MEXICO
DARE TO DREAM
LOVE DANGEROUSLY
REMEMBERED WITH LOVE
THE LUNDY SUMMER
A STRANGER RIDING
A HAUNTED AFFAIR
THE LOVE SEASON
WITHER THOU GOEST
A TOUCH OF MAGIC

PEGGY LOOSEMORE JONES

A SUMMER FOLLY

Complete and Unabridged

LINFORD
Leicester

First published in Great Britain in 1996

First Linford Edition
published 1999

Copyright © 1996 by Peggy Loosemore Jones

British Library CIP Data

Jones, Peggy Loosemore
    A summer folly.—Large print ed.—
Linford romance library
1. Love stories
2. Large type books
I. Title
823.9′14 [F]

ISBN 0–7089–5409–X

Published by
F. A. Thorpe (Publishing) Ltd.
Anstey, Leicestershire

Set by Words & Graphics Ltd.
Anstey, Leicestershire
Printed and bound in Great Britain by
T. J. International Ltd., Padstow, Cornwall

This book is printed on acid-free paper

1

All through her recital, Philippa felt the stranger's gaze upon her. She was becoming used to being watched while she played but this was a different, almost physical sensation and it was very disturbing.

Why is he so interested in me, she wondered.

She was performing in the chancel of the village church and the sun, striking low through the stained-glass window, lit up the gold-painted frame of her harp and gleamed on her bare arms.

The old church was full and the audience hushed as she brought her recital to a close with her own arrangement of 'Greensleeves.' The final cadence whispered and died somewhere in the vaulted roof and, after a moment, the applause came.

She stood to receive it, bowing

slightly and smiling at the local people she knew so well. Briefly she caught the eyes of the man in the second pew who had been watching her so intently — a tall, dark-haired man with heavy eyebrows and strong, bold features.

In his smart city suit he stood out among the villagers and although she did not recognise him, she guessed he was the man she'd been hearing about.

Philippa glanced quickly away for the vicar was speaking, thanking her for a delightful concert. Several people came up to compliment her on her performance afterwards. She saw that the stranger was waiting until they had all moved away, so she was ready for him when he came.

'Philippa Southcott?' he said and smiled. 'I enjoyed your recital. But you don't remember me, do you?'

He was more attractive when he smiled as his brooding expression softened.

'I'm sorry, I don't,' she said. And

yet — there was something about him. It was something that echoed from a long time ago. She read a question in his eyes and added, 'But as you're the only stranger here I assume you must be Alex Penfold.'

'Well done, Miss Southcott!' His eyes held a mocking glint now. 'If you don't remember me, I remember you, though it's a long time since I saw you last.'

'Oh?'

'Must be about ten years. I was seventeen and you were — about fourteen? Sure you don't remember?'

'Sorry!' she said, shaking her head.

'It was when I came down with my parents for my grandfather's funeral. Your mother and father called at the manor to pay their respects and brought you with them. The grown-ups told us to go outside while they talked so we went down to the woods and played hide-and-seek.' He lifted an eyebrow. 'You don't remember that?'

'No.' But thoughts were beginning to stir — of running in the woods with her hair flying — of laughing and being chased — and a kind of delicious terror.

'Not when you hid in the old hermitage and I crept up behind it and jumped in on you? I've never seen anyone so scared before!'

'Now I remember! How could I forget — you gave me such a fright!'

'Poor little Philippa!' He smiled. 'I'm sorry, I didn't mean to. But I said sorry afterwards. I wouldn't have done it if I thought I was really going to scare you.'

He reached out a hand to touch her hair, making Philippa jerk away in alarm. Alex had had a strange effect on her that day at the manor — he hadn't been like the others boys in the village. He seemed more mature and sure of himself.

'Anyway,' she said quickly, 'what are you doing here again?'

'I'm here for another funeral

unfortunately.' He regarded her intently.

'Yes, your uncle's, isn't it? We heard you were coming.'

'Nothing escapes the village, does it? Yes, I'm here to say goodbye to Uncle Arthur and find out what sort of mess he's left the estate in!'

Philippa frowned.

'I don't think there's much wrong with it.' There had been rumours in the village that this new young Penfold would be very different from old Mr Arthur and she wondered now if the rumours might be true.

'Oh, come on, Philippa!' Alex said. 'From what I hear, my uncle hadn't been looking after things properly. He was only really interested in his gardens!'

'The estate's been well managed,' she protested.

'Has it? We'll see. There will have to be plenty of changes when I take over.'

She stared at him.

5

'You're taking over?'

'According to the will I am. I'm the last of the Penfolds and even Uncle Arthur wasn't fool enough to let the estate go out of the family.'

'I see.' Philippa turned away from him and began collecting her music.

'I'll be at the manor for a while yet so we're sure to meet again.'

'I'm very busy.'

'With concerts?' He glanced at her harp. 'It must be awkward, lugging that thing around.'

Philippa stroked the spine of her harp with affection.

'It's no trouble. I have my trolley and I use my father's van. Jimmy's helping me tonight.'

'Jimmy?'

'Jimmy Laramy, your farm manager's son. You haven't met him?'

'I soon will. I've called a meeting of all the estate workers after the funeral tomorrow. I suppose this Jimmy works on the farm?'

'He helps out sometimes. But he's

mostly in charge of the Valley Gardens. They're very well known. People come from miles around to visit them.'

'Really?' Alex Penfold looked interested. 'And do they pay?'

'There's a charity box for donations.'

'A charity box!' He gave a sardonic laugh. 'Like I said, Philippa, there will have to be changes!'

She felt her cheeks flush.

'Good-night, Mr Penfold. I can see Jimmy coming in. He'll have brought the van to the church porch.'

'Then allow me!' Alex said. 'Where's your trolley? I'll lift your harp for you.'

She let him, begrudgingly, then saw, to her relief, that Jimmy was hurrying towards them. His cheerful, ruddy face was wreathed in smiles as he took charge of the harp and started trundling it down the aisle.

'A great concert, Philippa!' he said. 'Everybody's saying so. There were lots of pound coins and five pound notes in the plate.'

He looked enquiringly at Alex and

Philippa said, 'This is Mr Penfold, Jimmy. He's here for his uncle's funeral.'

'Oh, aye! Glad to meet you, sir! We heard you were coming.' Jimmy took Alex's hand in his own large one and gave it a hearty shake. 'He'll be missed round here, will your Uncle Arthur. He'd have been here tonight, making his contribution, if he hadn't been in a better place.'

Alex took out his wallet.

'In that case, I'd better do it for him.' He extracted three ten pound notes and dropped them into the collection plate when they reached it.

The vicar was waiting by the heavy oak door to say good-night and Philippa saw his eyes open wide. He swept down upon Alex at once.

'My dear sir,' she heard him say as she followed Jimmy outside. 'So generous!'

'Must be made of money, that one,' Jimmy remarked before he loaded the harp into the van.

'He was showing off. And he could be trouble.' Philippa sighed, suddenly feeling weary. 'Oh, take me home, Jimmy! I'm tired now.'

On the way to the cottage she shared with her father she told Jimmy how Alex Penfold was planning changes to the estate, changes she feared would not be for the better.

'As long as he doesn't touch the Valley Gardens! Mr Arthur's life work, they were.'

'Yes. Well, you'll find out what he has in mind when he talks to you all tomorrow.'

'After the funeral. Will you be in the church?'

'I'm rehearsing in Exeter. But I expect Father will go.'

'He didn't come to hear you tonight.'

'He had an order to complete. Anyway, he's heard me play often enough.'

'Your dad's still working hard,' Jimmy said when he drew up outside the Southcotts' cottage. 'The light's still on in his workshop.'

'He works too hard.' Philippa turned to Jimmy before she opened the van door. 'Coming in for coffee?'

'No. You're tired and your dad's busy. I'll get the harp inside for you and take myself off. I'd best get an early night to be upsides with Mr Penfold tomorrow!'

'Now you mustn't let him bully you!'

'No fear of that!' Jimmy grinned as he got out of the van. He unloaded the harp and wheeled it to the cottage porch. 'You watch you don't get taken in by him either!'

'Me?' Philippa stared at Jimmy.

'I could see he had his eye on you. And he'll think he's somebody now that he's lord of the manor. I wouldn't be surprised if he promised you the earth!'

'Now you're being silly!'

'Am I?' Jimmy's face was unusually serious when he looked at Philippa. They were much the same height and even though the porch was shadowy under its smothering of honeysuckle, there was still enough light for her to see the concern and tenderness in his blue eyes. He touched her arm. 'I wouldn't like to see you get hurt by a Penfold. There's bad blood in that family. Everybody says so.'

'That's just village gossip!'

'Well, you take care! We've been friends for a long time, Philippa, and I like to look out for you.'

'I know you do. But don't worry! Alex Penfold's not likely to stay around here for long and I'm away more often than I'm at home.' She opened the cottage door so that he could lift the harp over the porch step. 'Thanks for being such a help tonight.'

'Any time you need me, you just say! All right?'

'All right.' She kissed him lightly on the cheek. 'Good-night, Jimmy. Good luck for tomorrow.'

She watched him park the van close to the cottage wall and waved as he walked off down the hill. Then she wheeled her harp into the living-room which opened directly from the front door.

She lifted it from its trolley and stood it in the alcove to the right of the fireplace where it fitted and nicely balanced the china cabinet her father had made for her mother which filled the other alcove.

The conversation with Jimmy left her troubled because she knew the reason for it. He had been in love with her for years. They had grown up together and he had been her protector at the village school, fighting the older boys when they mocked her for having music lessons and called her posh when she was sent away to an academy in Exeter.

He was always there, welcoming her whenever she came home, devoted to her and expecting nothing more than friendship in return.

She sighed as she went up to the bedroom that had been hers since childhood. Quickly she changed from her formal dress into something more comfortable.

She stared at herself in the dressing-table mirror, seeing a tall, slim girl with wide-set, grey-green eyes and a mouth that turned up at the corners. There was a sprinkling of freckles over her nose and cheeks and her tawny hair fell around her face in natural curls. She went over to her window and looked out. It was getting dark now but she could just make out the roof of Penfold Manor down in the valley.

On the far horizon, the hills of Exmoor were silhouetted against the sky and winding around the estate there was the stretch of woodland that hid the little gothic hermitage where she had encountered Alex Penfold for the first time . . .

Forget it, she thought. And forget him! Moving abruptly from the window she went downstairs to look for her father.

He was still in his workshop at the

end of their garden but when she went in she saw that he was beginning to pack away his tools. His love of woodwork had started as a hobby but was now his business.

He had started off by making children's toys and dolls' house furniture but these days his pieces were collectors' items. He was beginning to receive orders from all over the world for his miniature antique tables and chairs, grandfather clocks that worked, Victorian dressers and china cabinets, rocking chairs and four-poster beds.

She went over to kiss him.

'All finished?'

He nodded.

'I'll get the parcel off in the morning. How was the concert?'

'It seemed to go down well. Lots of people came so the vicar was pleased.'

'I'm sorry I missed it.' Martin Southcott rubbed his eyes.

She saw that he was tired. His eyes were dark rimmed and his shoulders stooped from constantly bending over

14

his work bench. His hair was greying and beginning to recede. She felt a rush of affection for him as she took his arm.

'Come on! You must be ready for coffee. I know I am.' She waited while he locked the workshop and pocketed the key. 'Jimmy wouldn't stay,' she said as they were walking up the garden path. 'He has a heavy day tomorrow with the funeral. The gardens are supplying the flowers and Alex Penfold's called a meeting after it for all the estate workers.'

'He's here, then?'

'He was at the concert and said he remembered me from when we were younger.'

'Really?' They had reached the kitchen where Philippa moved to fill the kettle. 'I'm surprised at that,' Martin said. 'His side of the family's hardly ever been here since the quarrel.'

'There was a quarrel?'

'Between Alex's father and his Uncle Arthur — long before you were born. It was all over a girl — Elizabeth Ash. She was the village belle in those days.'

'You knew her?'

'She was a popular girl!' Martin chuckled. 'There was a sort of competition then — who could walk out with Lizzie Ash! But we knew we didn't stand a chance against the Penfold boys. Lizzie was housemaid at the manor and the rest of us reckoned they had an unfair advantage.'

'So what happened?'

'Arthur wanted to marry her but old Jacob Penfold soon put a stop to that. Lizzie wasn't good enough for his son and heir so he sent her packing. The next thing we knew she was having a baby and had run off with the brother, John!'

'Alex's father?'

'That's what they said. Whatever the truth of it, it caused an almighty row. The old man threatened to cut John out of his will and Arthur just went to pieces. He never looked at another woman and lost interest in everything except his gardens.'

Philippa filled and switched on the kettle.

'So that's why Alex was here all those years ago and met me! He said he was down with his parents for his grandfather's funeral.'

'That's right! I remember now. I wonder if he's brought Lizzie with him this time.'

'He was on his own in the church. I suppose they wanted to find out where they stood when they were here before. Were they cut out of the will?'

'John was. Arthur was in line for the estate, anyway. I believe the money that should have gone to John was left in trust for young Alex until he was twenty-one. He's got the lot now because his father died a few years ago and he's the last of the Penfolds.'

And out to make changes, Philippa recalled. So how will that affect the village? How will it affect us all?

2

Philippa set off with her harp early the next morning in her father's old van. The rehearsal in Exeter was with an orchestra largely made up from the university's music students with a backbone of seasoned amateur musicians and paid professionals.

She was looking forward to it as there were exciting plans to tour the county and she enjoyed orchestral work more than solo recitals.

But her mind was not on her music as she drove through the narrow Devon lanes towards the Exeter road. She was thinking instead of Arthur Penfold who was being buried that morning and who had devoted his life to creating his beautiful gardens after the woman he loved had married his brother.

And she was remembering Arthur's forceful young nephew who could so easily sweep all that work away and change the estate that had been the focus of village life for centuries.

Perhaps he won't change it, she thought, as she drove into Exeter. When he sees the Valley Gardens and how well the estate has been kept, perhaps he'll just put somebody in charge and go away, leaving everything as it is.

But there had been determination in Alex's dark eyes when he'd said, 'There will have to be changes.' She shivered. I must stop thinking about him, she told herself. I've more important things in hand, this rehearsal for a start.

It lasted much longer than she expected, spreading over into the afternoon so it was almost supper time before she arrived back home.

Her father was not in the cottage or his workshop but as he sometimes went for a drink in the evenings she walked down to the local inn to look for him.

He was at the centre of a group

of men in a corner of the bar and she saw that Jimmy and his father were there with the stockman and a couple of labourers from the farm. They were in heated discussion when she went over.

'Ah, Pippa!' her father said. 'You're back! What can I get you?'

'A lager and lime, if you're offering.' She regarded the glum faces of the other men. 'What's going on? You're looking very serious.'

'So would you be,' Jimmy said, 'if you'd been listening to the mighty Penfold all afternoon. Do you know what he wants to do with the estate?'

'I can't imagine! Tell me!'

'He wants to turn it into a theme park!'

'What?' Philippa gave an incredulous laugh.

'He's talking about doing up the manor and putting on eighteenth-century banquets with everybody dressed up. And he wants part of the farm to look like it was a couple of hundred years ago with horses instead of tractors and a lot of old tools and implements on show!'

'Would you have to dress up, too?' Philippa could not help grinning.

'Over my dead body!' Jimmy said, glowering. 'It's not funny, Pippa!'

'Sorry. I just had a mental picture of you all wearing smocks and straw hats.' Nobody laughed and she tried to keep a straight face. 'So what about the Valley Gardens?'

'He's leaving them for now. But in time he'd like them more formal, more eighteenth century. He even wants a maze! And he'd turn some of the farm buildings into places for arts and crafts and a shop. The bloke's mad!'

The other men growled agreement and Jimmy's father broke in.

'The manor farm's always been sheep and cattle but he's talking about bringing back some of the old breeds.'

'Can you still get the old breeds?' Philippa asked.

'Oh, there's plenty of Exmoor Horns running the moors,' Jeff said. 'The Devon Rubies are scarce but they're still about. But they don't come cheap.'

'Money's no object to him,' Jimmy said. 'He was on about opening up the woods for a carriageway so that his visitors could drive round the estate in a pony and trap!'

Philippa's father brought over her drink from the bar.

'Delusions of grandeur!' he remarked. 'The inheritance has gone to his head.'

'Of course the manor is eighteenth century,' Philippa pointed out.

'Built around seventeen forty,' Martin said. 'Arthur Penfold never did much to keep it in repair so I can see young Alex might want to do it up a bit.'

'He can do what he likes to the manor!' Jimmy said. 'If he wants to live in it, that's his look-out. But he'd better lay off the farm and the gardens!'

'He's going to live there?' Philippa was astonished. 'Did he say so?'

'Well, it sounded like it. He said

he was bringing his mother down to run the place. Can't think what Peggy Tucker'll say. She's been housekeeper there for years.'

'Can't think what folk in Penworth will say, either,' Jimmy's father growled, 'if Lizzie Ash shows her face around here again!'

'That's hardly fair, Jeff!' Martin said sharply.

'Well, what d'you expect? She didn't turn up for the funeral, did she? I can tell you one thing. I don't feel like bowing and scraping to the bountiful Lizzie Ash! I don't suppose Peggy Tucker does, either.'

'Expecting a tidy bit in Mr Arthur's will, Peggy was,' Jimmy said, 'but didn't get a penny.'

There was a gloomy silence while the men drank their beer. Philippa could see from her father's face that Jeff Laramy's remarks about Lizzie had angered him. As for herself, she was marvelling at what she had just been told.

Changes, Alex Penfold had said, but she had not expected anything so bizarre. Was he really going to live in the manor? He would be harder to avoid if he was right on her doorstep!

'I can't understand where he's got all these ideas from,' she said at last. 'He doesn't seem the type to be so interested in the past.'

'Oh, he's done this sort of thing before!' Jimmy exploded. 'It's his line of business, what he calls the heritage industry! Theme parks, tarted up country houses, you name it and he's in it! He'll start on this pub next, you'll see! It still belongs to the estate and so do a lot of the cottages. You pay rent to the manor, don't you, Mr Southcott?'

'Well, yes, I do,' Philippa's father admitted.

'Better watch out, then!' Jeff growled. 'He'll be upping your rent or wanting you out to make room for an eighteenth-century coachman, or some such! I reckon all us locals ought to get together

24

and put a stop to this before it goes too far!' He threw back his head and emptied his glass. 'Who's for another?'

'No more for me,' Martin Southcott said. He glanced at Philippa. 'You must be hungry, so we'll go when you're ready.'

On the way back to the cottage she and her father were both thoughtful. Philippa did not really believe their tenancy of the cottage would be affected or that all of Alex Penfold's ambitious plans would bear fruit. What bothered her most was the way old scandals were being revived and the bad feeling Alex had already stirred up between himself and his workers on the estate.

After supper Philippa felt restless. It was a beautiful evening with still an hour or two of light so she walked up the hill to the churchyard where Arthur Penfold had been buried that morning. The piled earth of his grave was covered in bunches of flowers brought by the villagers and in the centre of it there lay a large wreath of roses, freshly picked from his beloved gardens.

Jimmy did well, she thought and was reading some of the cards attached to the flowers when she heard a step on the gravelled path behind her. She turned to see Alex Penfold.

'I didn't expect to find you here,' he said.

'I couldn't get to the funeral this morning.'

'So you're paying your last respects now?' He looked down at his uncle's grave. 'I only met my Uncle Arthur once so I've built up a picture of him from things I was told. I was surprised to see so many villagers in the church today.'

'He was well respected.'

'Perhaps I've misjudged him, then. Anyway, I felt I owed him more than I was able to give him this morning, so that's why I'm here just now.'

'I often come,' Philippa said. 'It's so peaceful here. My mother's buried underneath that cherry tree.'

'I remember her,' Alex said and smiled. 'She was very cross with me that day because I kept you out for so long. Are you going over to her grave?'

'Not tonight.' If he had not been there she would have done and lingered for a while. But he made her feel self-conscious and would have intruded on her memories.

'I had a walk round the estate this afternoon,' he said, 'after my meeting with the workmen. The woods are overgrown but the hermitage is still there.'

'I know.'

'You've been there since?'

'A few times — on my way to the farm.'

'To see Jimmy Laramy?'

'We're old friends.'

'I gathered that.' He frowned. 'The Laramys weren't very friendly today.'

'Weren't they?' She made a move towards the gate. 'I must get back, Mr Penfold. My father will wonder where I am.'

'Wait!' He put a hand on her arm. 'I didn't make a very good start with the men this afternoon and I'd like to think there's somebody in the village I can call a friend. For old times' sake, Philippa?'

'We were much younger, then!' she objected. 'I didn't see you again so I forgot all about you!'

'Did you? All the more reason for me to remind you now, then! Walk down to the woods with me this evening! I'd like your advice on what to do about the hermitage. I've plans to open up the woods for a carriageway and it's in quite the wrong place.'

'You wouldn't get rid of it?'

'No. Just move it if that's possible.'

'But you'd spoil it! You couldn't dismantle all those hundreds of stones and put them together again properly!' she burst out. 'No wonder you didn't make a good start with the men! Most of your ideas sounded like a joke but this is too much!'

'They've been talking, have they?'

'Of course they have! They're worried and so am I! You can't just barge in and start tearing the place apart! Do you really imagine Penworth folk will stand by and let you turn the estate into a theme park?'

'There's not much they could do to stop me! But don't look so cross, Philippa! I'm open to suggestions. So why not walk down there with me now and let me tell you what I have in mind?'

'I know already! You want to cheapen Penfold Manor to make money out of it — dress it up in the past and turn your workers into peasants! But they're not peasants, Mr Penfold, as you'll soon find out!'

'Threats, Philippa? You'd better warn your friends I won't take too kindly to that. I want to keep them on if they co-operate, but I'm not a charity. The place will have to earn its keep and so will they.'

She saw she had gone too far and bit back an angry retort. She did not want to get Jimmy and the other men into trouble.

'They're good workers,' she said, 'and they look on the manor as much their heritage as yours. Anyway, you don't need to give it a mock history. It has one of its own.'

'I know that. I'd just like to build on it — paint it up a little.'

'It would be a fake, don't you see? Nobody would be taken in by it.'

'It's just for entertainment, Philippa! The general public like that sort of thing, especially the Americans and the Japanese.'

'Oh!' She threw her arms up. 'It's no use talking to you!'

'It would put Penworth on the map!'

Pippa was already walking away. 'It doesn't want to be on the map!' she shouted over her shoulder. 'It likes being where it is, where it's always been!'

'You can't stop progress, Philippa!'

No, she thought. But perhaps we can stop you. We should form a united front, the way Jeff Laramy suggested! But when she put that idea to her father on her return to the cottage, he was not enthusiastic.

'Keep out of it, Pippa!' he advised. 'It's an estate matter.'

'But we're part of the estate — or the cottage is!'

'He won't interfere with us.'

'How can you be sure! Anyway, it isn't just the estate. It's the whole village. If he goes ahead with his theme park we'll be invaded.'

'It hasn't happened yet, so don't worry!' Martin changed the subject. 'How was the rehearsal today?'

'I enjoyed it. The concerts start soon, the first one's in Exeter. And I met up with a girl called Sarah who was at the academy with me. She plays the flute and she wants us to give some recitals together.'

'Good!' Martin gazed at his daughter fondly. 'You're going to be too busy to bother about the estate. Leave it to the Laramys and the rest of them to fight it out with young Alex! It won't hurt them to be shaken up a bit. They had it easy for years with Mr Arthur. He just let them get on with it and put all his energies into his gardens.'

Which is more or less what Alex said, Philippa thought. She wondered if she should have let him tell her more about his ideas. But the prospect of walking down to the hermitage with him had been too alarming. The quickening of her pulse and the look in his eyes had warned her that she was attracted and that he was, too. It was as if something drew them together, something she would have to struggle against if it were not to interfere with her music.

So I shall make sure I keep well out of your way, Alex Penfold, she resolved, because I have important plans for my life and they do not include you!

But it seemed he was not going to be so easily avoided, for the next morning Alex called very early at the cottage and Philippa answered the door to him.

3

Philippa was so amazed to see Alex it was a moment before she found her voice.

'Oh!' she said. 'Are you looking for me?'

'No. Your father. I'm checking on my properties in the village to see if they're in good repair.'

'Father's in his workshop. Shall I fetch him?' She moved to let him in.

'Don't bother! I'll take a quick look round and have a word with him afterwards. Any problems, Philippa? The thatch is looking a big shabby. Not leaking, is it?'

'Not that I know of.' She felt self-conscious, bothered by his presence in their living-room.

'Then I'll pop upstairs first,' he said. 'No need to come with me.'

She watched him climb the narrow,

twisting staircase which led up from a corner of the room and listened as he moved around above her. It was a good few minutes before she heard him come down the stairs again.

'There's just this room, down here, the kitchen and the scullery,' she told him. 'Oh, and Father's workshop in the garden. I think everything's all right.'

'Good!' He began prowling round the room, tapping the walls and examining the fireplace. Some of her father's best pieces of miniature furniture were displayed in the china cabinet and he paused to peer at them. 'This is your father's work, isn't it? Does he manage to sell much of it?'

'He does now. It was hard at first, but he's beginning to build up a reputation. He gets orders from all over the place.' She felt a swelling of pride. 'These are collectors' items now, Mr Penfold.'

'I can see that. But there's no need to be so formal, Philippa. Surely you can call me Alex?' He was still engrossed in contemplating Martin's work. 'I might be able to put some work your father's way.'

'He's got more than he can cope with already!'

'I'm sure your father won't want to turn down an opportunity, Philippa. I think he should be making that decision.'

'Perhaps we're not all so keen on making money as you are!'

'But you're ambitious, surely?' Alex raised his eyebrows. 'I've been hearing all about you — passing your exams and winning awards.'

'That's different. It's my career.'

'And mine's making money. It had to be. My father died young and Uncle Arthur did nothing for Mother and me. As soon as I got hold of my grandfather's legacy I had to make it work for us. Now I've a nice little business going.'

'Part of the heritage industry?'

He missed the mockery in her voice.

'I saw an opening and I took it.

I'm a consultant, Philippa — an ideas man. People come to me with vague plans and I find the experts to make them work. Of course, my name has helped.'

'Because you're a Penfold?'

'Yes. I'm not above making use of that. The family treated my father very badly and all I'm trying to do is gain back some of the dignity he lost.'

Philippa flushed.

'Yes, I can see that you probably are.'

He began to move towards the kitchen.

'Then let's get this over with. I'll have a word with your father. After that, I'd like you to think again about taking a look at the hermitage and coming along to the manor with me.'

'I was going to spend the morning practising.'

'I've a proposition to put to you, anyway,' he said, walking into the kitchen. 'A possible music engagement.'

'I've a lot on just now.' Philippa was cautious.

'It wouldn't be for a while.' He was frowning at their old-fashioned stone sink with its wooden draining board. 'You could do with a replacement here. Stainless steel, perhaps.'

'We like this old one. It's always been there.'

'It's chipped, Philippa. Very unhygienic!' He scribbled in his notebook. 'I'll mention it to your father. Will you come to the manor with me afterwards?'

She hesitated. His face was giving nothing away so she could not tell what his motive was — if the music engagement was an opportunity, or just a bait.

'All right,' she said at last. 'But I can't stay long.'

He was so long talking to her father, she had started playing her harp before he reappeared. For a moment he listened from the doorway and it was not until she looked up that she saw him.

'Oh! I thought you might have gone off to inspect the rest of your properties,' she said.

'No. They can wait.' He came over to her and stared critically at her harp. 'I suppose a harp must cost an awful lot of money.'

'My father bought it for me out of his redundancy money. That's why I'm so keen to make a success of my career.'

'I see.' He frowned. 'Does that mean you want to carry on practising and not come to the manor with me?'

'No. I said I'd come. I just don't like wasting time.' She lifted her harp back into its corner. 'You and Father must have found plenty to talk about.'

'I've been watching him work. He's an artist, Philippa. But he's no businessman, is he? He's selling his work far too cheaply.'

'He's still making his way, so he's satisfied.'

'For all the hours he puts in? I could help him, if he'd let me.'

'He wouldn't.' She moved to the door. 'But don't let's start arguing about money again! Half the morning's gone already. I'll still have to finish practising when I come back.'

As they walked he asked about her concerts with the Exeter orchestra, sounding genuinely interested. He even promised to try to attend one of the performances, although she doubted if he was really serious about that.

Just as they reached the wrought-iron gates of the drive he said, 'When I go back to London, I'll be contacting a few people who put money into some of my ventures. I'm going to invite them down for a week-end so they can get a better idea of the estate and what I plan to do with it. I won't be ready to put on a banquet for them, but I could manage a dinner. I wondered if you'd like to come and play for us.'

'They'd never listen!' she scoffed. 'Not if they'd come to talk business.'

'But you'd be able to help with that. You'd create the right atmosphere

39

if you played some eighteenth-century music.'

'And dressed up, too, I suppose! No thanks! If I come, I'll be strictly myself and play what I want to play.'

'Agreed.' She saw the triumph in his eyes again and realised she had fallen into a trap. 'I'll leave all that to you as long as you'll come.'

He opened the gates and they began walking up the long drive to Penfold Manor. It was an imposing building, gleaming white in the sunshine, double-fronted and austerely Georgian with the gold-painted family crest standing out high on the wall above the pillared porch.

'Come in for coffee before we go down to the hermitage,' Alex said. 'I told Mrs Tucker to expect us.'

'Before you knew I'd come?'

'Because I was sure you would.' He took her arm. 'I associate you with the estate, Philippa. You've always been mixed up with it in my memories.'

He took her hand and led her up

the steps to the heavy oak door and pushed it open.

'So, welcome back,' he said as he ushered her into the entrance hall. 'Make yourself a part of my memories again.'

She knew at once she had been there before, even though she thought she had forgotten the place.

'Come into the morning-room,' he said. 'I'll tell Peggy Tucker we're here.'

The room seemed much too full of pink velvet armchairs. There were two sofas in the same colour, several occasional tables and cabinets and a black fireplace with white columns, filled now with fir cones.

When he came back, he said, 'Make yourself at home, Philippa! Coffee's on the way. I've something to show you.'

He pulled one of the tables close to the sofa, indicated that she should sit beside him and spread a plan over the table top.

'This will give you some idea of what I have in mind.'

The manor itself would remain structurally the same, he told her, but there would have to be some interior alterations like the installation of central heating and extra bathrooms, complete redecoration and changes to the furniture.

'Some of the stuff here is junk,' he said. 'I'd like the house to look as near to eighteenth century again, but my guests will have to be comfortable.'

'What about the farm?' Philippa asked.

'The farmhouse is OK but I'm having the roof stripped of slate and put back into thatch. I know we can't really return to the eighteenth century, sheep have to be dipped these days, but I want to bring back some of the old breeds like the Exmoor Longhorns and there's no reason why some of them couldn't be sheared by hand. We could even have somebody spinning the wool and dyeing it because I plan to turn any outbuildings not being used into workshops for village crafts, that sort of thing. What d'you think?'

'Well — ' Philippa stared at the plan. 'It's very ambitious.' She pointed to a blocked-in area near Arthur Penfold's gardens. 'What's this?'

'That's where I'd like a maze. They're very popular again and I know a man who designs them.'

'Surely a maze would take years to grow?' Philippa said.

Alex shook his head.

'Not any longer. They can be made very quickly now from brick and turf. I don't want one that's too big or too difficult — just something the public can get round in about half an hour with an interesting feature in the middle.'

'Such as — '

'Well — I was wondering about the hermitage.'

'Oh, no! You can't move it, Alex! It belongs in the woods!'

'It's just a folly! A nineteenth-century piece of nonsense, not historically in keeping with the manor at all.'

'So? What about your maze? That would be a twentieth-century piece of nonsense!'

He laughed.

'I haven't finally decided about the hermitage. But I would like to open up the woods for a carriageway again. There was one there once. The penfold ladies used it to drive around the estate.' He looked up as Peggy Tucker came into the room. 'But here's our coffee. Thanks, Mrs Tucker.'

Peggy Tucker did not smile back. She slammed her tray down on to the table and walked out of the room without a word.

'She's becoming impossible.' Alex frowned. 'I'll have to get rid of her if she goes on like this.'

'Why? What's she done?' Philippa was dismayed.

'Taken a huff because I told her I'm bringing my mother down to take charge. If she can't adapt, she'll have to go!'

'But she's been here for years!'

Philippa poured the coffee, feeling resentment rising.

'That's the trouble! She's ruled the roost for far too long!'

'But don't you see? It's this high-handed attitude that's annoying the locals. Why can't you treat them more reasonably?'

'I don't want her upsetting my mother. She's had enough to put up with.'

At that, Philippa bit back a retort and softened her approach.

'My father knew your mother when she was a girl. He said she was the village belle.'

'So I've heard. But it didn't do her much good!'

'Will she mind coming back here?'

'She's not keen,' he said. 'Village scandal lasts for generations. But she'll do it for me.'

He seemed so confident Philippa felt a tremor of warning. If his mother so easily did his bidding, might he expect other women to do the same?

'Has she any family left in Penworth?' she asked.

'No. They moved away. Couldn't stand the talk.'

He was silent for a moment. Then he started telling her how he had been looking up the family records in his uncle's library and had found plans for an eighteenth-century garden he hoped to use when he got round to altering the Valley Gardens.

'The locals wouldn't stand for that! Your uncle spent most of his life creating them and they're perfect the way they are. Have you been down there?'

'Only briefly.'

'Then take a proper look! Ask Jimmy to show you round! He knows almost as much about them as your uncle did.'

'It seems to me the Laramys know too much about everything! His father's already dead set against my re-introducing any of the old breeds.'

'That's because he's familiar with the

ones that do well here!'

'Then he should think again! I discovered something else in the records, Philippa. My great-great-grandfather built up the finest herd of Devon Ruby-red cattle in the county. So don't tell me they didn't do well here! Just think how pleased he'd be if he knew I hoped to bring them back again!'

That silenced Philippa and she listened as he outlined his vision for the estate. She realised for the first time that there was more to it than just making money. He was a Penfold and he was claiming his birthright, linking himself in his own way to the family that had renounced his father and despised his mother. Understanding this, she made no objection when he suggested that they should walk down to the woods together.

They followed the Pen stream from the bottom of the grassy bank until it led them to the dark tunnel that was the entrance to the woods. The path was so overgrown the trees met overhead in a tangle of branches and it all looked even more threatening than Philippa remembered. She hesitated for a moment before following Alex into the gloom. But the hermitage was not too far away.

It seemed smaller somehow. Some of the decorative slates on its pointed roof had been replaced by ones of a different pattern, but its circular wall with the two arched entrances was still sound, all the dovetailed stones in place.

'Who built it?' Philippa asked. 'Did you find out from the old records?'

'Whoever he was, he wasn't a hermit! One of the Penfold ladies had it made to use as a sort of summer house. Rumour has it she met her lover here.'

'Really?' Philippa did not dare to meet Alex's eyes.

'Romantic, isn't it? It's probably been used for the same purpose lots of times since then.' He held out a hand in invitation. 'So will you risk stepping inside it with me?'

She knew she should refuse but it

was as if something drew her towards the place, something that set her senses tingling and made her reach out to take Alex's hand. He pulled her gently towards him and before she could stop him, she felt his mouth warm against hers. Then his grip tightened and his kisses became more and more urgent as he swept her up into a passionate embrace that left her breathless.

'Well?' he whispered when he released her at last.

'That wasn't really meant to happen,' she said, flushed and shaken.

'But I was sure it would.' Alex smiled. 'When I saw you in church the other evening and realised that after all these years we'd managed to meet again, I knew it was inevitable.'

'Nothing's inevitable, Alex!'

'You don't believe in Fate?' he persisted.

'Not if you mean something planned out for us in advance. We make our own destiny, or I like to think we do.'

'You didn't have to come to the manor with me today. You needn't have come into the hermitage — '

'Perhaps I shouldn't have!'

'But you couldn't refuse, could you? It's no good, Philippa. We're meant for one another, don't you see?'

'No!' she cried. 'I don't believe that! And I'm not staying here a minute longer! I don't care what you do with the hermitage or the estate. You can do what you like, Alex Penfold!'

She heard him laughing as she began running back along the woodland path. When she came out into the sunshine again her heart was hammering. What is happening to me, she wondered. Why am I letting myself become involved with this man when I have so many more important things to do with my life?

4

Philippa was kept so busy with her music during the next few days she had little time to think about Alex. News of what he was doing filtered through to her when her father met Jimmy and the other men in the Penworth Arms. They were biding their time, but the Laramys were already incensed at hearing that the roof of their farmhouse was to be stripped of its slate and put back into thatch.

An agricultural historian had been spotted prowling about the farm and a builder had twice been seen with Alex, surveying the outbuildings.

'They were poking about in the pub as well,' Martin told Philippa. 'Nobody knows what for but they had a good look round and took a lot of notes.'

Exasperated, Philippa said, 'Why can't he go more slowly and take one thing at a time? He's upsetting everybody!'

'He's off to London at the week-end, expecting the central heating to be installed by the time he gets back in a couple of weeks. Peggy Tucker doesn't know if she's coming or going!'

'She's still there, then?'

'Up to now. He can't leave the place without somebody in charge.'

'Perhaps he'll being his mother back with him.'

And what will happen then, Philippa wondered, regretting her promise to play at the dinner for his business friends.

On the Friday evening before he set off for London, Alex called unexpectedly at the cottage looking for the dates and venues of her orchestral concerts so that he could be sure of attending one of the performances and could also arrange his dinner when it would not clash with her other engagements.

'I need you there, Philippa,' he said, 'and not just for your music. I'd like you to be my partner for the evening.'

'Oh? I didn't realise that was part of the contract!'

She caught a flash of what might have been hurt in his eyes before he said, 'Part of our friendship, I'd hoped.'

Ashamed of her sharpness she asked, more gently, 'Won't your mother be here by then? Surely she should partner you that evening?'

'If she's here, she'll be busy. In any case, I need you with me, Philippa. You must know why.'

'No, I don't know why!' she shot back. 'So please don't try to tell me! If I come to your dinner it'll be just to play for your guests and nothing more!'

'Are you absolutely sure about that?' He raised an eyebrow.

'Yes, I am! So don't push it, Alex!'

He laughed then and held out a hand.

'All right. I can wait. Good luck with your concerts. I'll be in the audience at one of them.'

She did not believe he would be and in the rush of final rehearsals she forgot all about his promise. The tour was planned over ten days, travelling around the South West with performances in the towns that had halls large enough to accommodate them. They were playing in the Queens Theatre in Barnstaple when she suddenly knew he was there.

She could not lift her eyes from her music to search for him but once the work was over and the conductor motioned them to stand for the applause, she looked up at the balcony and saw him in the front row.

He raised his hand and smiled down at her and she knew that she would never be able to escape him. If there was already such a bond between them that she could sense his presence, what hope was there for her? He was waiting outside the theatre when she went out to the coach with the other members of the orchestra.

'A wonderful concept, Philippa,' he said. 'Where are you all off to now?'

'The Imperial Hotel. We're staying overnight.'

'Then can I join you for a drink before you turn in?'

'I'm much too tired, Alex. We're off to Bude early in the morning so I must get to bed.' She saw his disappointment and added, 'I'm sorry. Are you back at the manor now?'

'I'm on my way. I just stopped off for the concert and I'm glad I did. I'll see you next week in Penworth, then.'

'Perhaps.' She glanced at the coach and realised that nearly everybody was aboard. 'I must go, Alex. They're waiting for me.'

'But so am I!' He moved closer and, before she realised what he intended, had caught her by the shoulders and kissed her on the lips. It was a long kiss, firm but tender, and her heart was racing when he let her go. 'I told you I could wait,' he murmured. 'But try not to make it much longer, Philippa!'

Her face felt hot when she climbed into the coach and met the curious eyes of the other members of the orchestra. Sarah Barnes, her friend who played the flute, had saved her a seat.

'Who was that?' she asked as Philippa slid in beside her.

'Just a man I know.'

'Important?'

'No!'

'Better watch out, then! He looked as if he means business.'

Philippa said nothing for she had thought much the same. But what is he really expecting of me, she wondered. Remembering his passionate kisses in the hermitage and her own instinctive response to them she shivered, realising exactly what he was expecting.

When she returned to the village she found that things had moved on. There was a brand new sink unit in their kitchen which she hated on sight and her father told her that the builders had completed the installation of the central heating at the manor and started on the bathrooms. Alex's mother had arrived and was very firmly in charge.

'It sounds as if she's still the same Lizzie.' Martin chuckled. 'She was a lively one in the old days. According to Jimmy she put Peggy Tucker in her place straightaway.'

'Was there much trouble between them?'

'If there was, it's over and Peggy's staying on. They're having a furniture sale there on Saturday to get rid of a lot of the old stuff. Half the village will be going. I thought I'd look in and see if there's any decent wood I could use. Want to come with me? You need a couple of days to relax. We could stroll through the gardens afterwards. Jimmy tells me the rhododendrons are a picture.'

So Saturday saw Martin and Philippa joining a crowd of other villagers on their way to Penfold Manor. The sale was being held in one of the barns and there was an hour's viewing time before the auctioneer was due.

The furniture on show was mostly pre-war or poor reproduction and not very exciting. But Philippa found a pretty armchair she liked and her father thought he might bid for two bookcases he could cut down. There was such a crush in the barn that they stepped outside again until the sale should begin. While they were waiting in the sunshine, Philippa saw Alex coming across the farm track towards them with the auctioneer and a woman she did not know.

'Look, Dad!' she said. 'Is that Mrs Penfold?'

'I believe it is. Well! Lizzie certainly hasn't altered all that much!'

Alex was making straight for them.

'Philippa!' he said. 'I didn't realise you were back. Have you come to buy?'

'Perhaps.' Philippa smiled at the woman beside him, a striking woman with Alex's bold good looks and something of the gipsy in her dark hair and eyes.

'This is my mother,' Alex said. 'Mother, meet Philippa Southcott and her father.'

'Hello, Martin,' Mrs Penfold said and held out a hand. 'It's been a long time.'

'But I'd have known you anywhere,' he said. 'Nice to have you back, Lizzie!'

'I see you two are old friends,' Alex said. 'You'll have a lot to catch up on.' He turned to Philippa. 'So why don't we leave them to it? I'd like to show you what's being done in the manor. Or would you prefer to go into the sale?'

'Well, that's what I've come for!'

'I'm sure your father can bid for anything you want. And Mother will keep an eye on things for me.' He slapped the auctioneer on the shoulder. 'Everything's in good hands here.'

'Father and I were going to take a walk in the gardens afterwards,' Philippa objected as Alex bustled her away.

'I'll take you there later.' He took

her arm. 'It's good to have you back! I've missed you and I want to know what you think of the alterations.'

'Why? What I think doesn't make the slightest difference! Our new kitchen sink looks ghastly.'

'Then choose another one you'd like instead!'

His exuberance alarmed her and the way he took charge, sweeping everything before him, regardless of other people's opinions. She could see that his forcefulness would stand him in good stead in the world of business but feared it would never do in Penworth. All the same she had to admit that the alterations to the manor were being tastefully done.

Alex insisted on taking her all over the house and she was astonished at the number of rooms. The entrance hall led into a larger, inner hall from which an elegant dining-room opened at one side and a well-stocked library from the other. A curving staircase swept up from the middle of the hall to a wide landing where the walls were hung with landscape paintings and portraits of the Penfold ancestors. There were eight bedrooms and two of them were in the process of being equipped with their own bathrooms, really more like boudoirs with their elegant wash basins set into old-fashioned wash stands and free-standing baths with curved legs.

A second, back staircase led down from what had once been the servants' quarters and there was still a line of summoning bells on the wall outside the stone-flagged kitchen.

'It's all so big!' Philippa marvelled. 'When d'you think you'll be ready for your first guests?'

'Early August with luck. I mean to catch the end of the summer season.'

'You're in a hurry!'

'Yes.' She saw the determination in his eyes. 'I've spent my working life realising other people's dreams, Philippa. This one's all mine and it's got to be a success!'

There was something obsessive about

the way he spoke and she felt uneasy.

'I hope you won't be disappointed, then,' she said. 'Things don't always work out the way we'd like.'

'They do if we want them badly enough. There are two things I mean to have. The first is my proper place here at Penfold with the estate restored the way I intend it to be.'

'And the second?'

'Ah!' His eyes gleamed. 'I'll keep that under wraps for a while! I promised I'd take you to the gardens.'

The glint in his eyes warned her that she might be the second thing he was determined to have. Her uneasiness increased.

'I think I'd rather see if Father's got what he was after at the sale.'

'That won't be over for ages!'

He was already leading her out by the back way from the kitchen where there was a short cut to the deep valley Arthur Penfold had transformed after his disappointment in love. She was troubled by the thought that Alex might be in danger of doing something similar if he became so obsessed with the estate he had no time for more important things in life. If he was looking on her as just another desirable possession she should make it clear she was not interested.

Yet when he put his arm round her on their way to the gardens she felt the same tingle of expectation as when he had led her into the hermitage and a similar helplessness which made it impossible for her to draw back.

Fool, she told herself and deliberately pulled away from him to run on ahead when they came in sight of the garden entrance. Once inside it, Philippa caught her breath and stood for a moment, taking in the feast of colour spread out before her.

On that late June afternoon the rhododendrons blazed in a glory of pinks, reds and purples and the lilacs and wisterias were heavy with blossom.

'It's so beautiful!' Philippa sighed when Alex caught her up. 'And so natural! Look at it! You mustn't change it!'

'I'd sooner look at you,' he murmured and put his arm round her again. 'Why did you run away from me, Philippa?'

'Oh, do be serious, Alex!' She shrugged off his arm. 'I didn't come here for that!'

'So what did you come for?'

'To make you appreciate how much the garden means to everybody! People are proud of what your uncle did and the men who've worked here would never forgive you if you changed it!'

'Men like Jimmy Laramy, I suppose!' Alex's lips set in a stubborn line. 'Uncle Arthur's dead, Philippa. Whoever works for me will have to take my orders or move on.'

'You'd surely talk things over with them?'

'Do these gardens mean so much to you?'

'Of course they do! I've grown up with them. I've watched everything your uncle did, every new piece of land he took over. Come down to the lakes! I'll show you my favourite place, the little heather grotto he made in that rocky corner behind the rose garden.'

'In a minute.' He drew her to him again. 'You're more beautiful to me than all Uncle Arthur's flowers. And so much more desirable.'

'That's enough, Alex! Don't say those things!'

'Why not? What are you afraid of, Philippa?'

She knew what she was afraid of, just as she had known when he had kissed her in the hermitage. Agitated, she began trying to pull him along the top path. But he only laughed and drew her to him again, holding her close and whispering such endearments in her ear her face flamed.

Then the sound of wheels on the pebbled path made them spring apart just as Jimmy Laramy came round the corner, trundling a cart full of compost. He stared at them both, taking in Philippa's obvious embarrassment. Then he gave a curt nod and pushed his cart past them without a word.

'Jimmy!' she called after him but he walked on as if he had not heard.

'He's not very friendly today, is he?' Alex commented.

She rounded on him then a sudden burst of anger.

'If you want your men to be friendly you'll have to treat them differently! They're experienced workers and they know this land a lot better than you do!'

'That doesn't make any difference.' Alex was clearly taken aback. 'It's time for a change, Philippa. I've told them I'll be getting advice from experts.'

'Good! Then you won't need any from me!' She swung away from him. 'I'm going back to the sale. I'd sooner come to the gardens on my own or with somebody who appreciates them!'

'Like your friend, Jimmy?'

'Why not?'

Ignoring his amazement she left him

standing there and hurried back the way they had come, furious with herself. She knew that her sudden outburst had been caused not only by the reproach she had read in Jimmy's eyes but also by her growing uncertainty as to where her loyalties lay.

5

Philippa went to church the next morning with her father and was pleased to see Jimmy in his usual seat. She knew she had to speak to him afterwards as she could not bear there to be bad feeling between them.

Just before the service began there was a ripple of movement among the congregation and when she looked round she saw Alex Penfold coming in with his mother. He made straight for the pew behind her and murmured. 'Good morning, Philippa,' in her ear before he sat down.

When the service was over and everyone stood up to go, Martin started chatting to Alex's mother which detained Alex as well. So Philippa murmured an apology and hurried after Jimmy who was already in the church porch.

He looked embarrassed when she approached him.

'What was the matter with you, yesterday?' she asked.

'You should know, Philippa. I thought you were on our side.'

'I am. But it doesn't help to be rude to your boss.'

'Was that why you let him kiss you?'

It was her turn to blush. 'He was messing about, that's all. I only went there to make him see how much the gardens mean to everybody and to get him to appreciate your point of view. Perhaps you should try to see his sometime.'

'He's getting round you, then, is he?'

'No! I just think you should give him a chance. Tell him when you believe he's wrong but at least listen. He's not a monster.'

'He's a Penfold, Philippa. There's a bad one in every generation. Lizzie Ash could tell you that!'

'She hasn't done too badly out of them!'

'So it seems! She's got a nerve, coming back here! Penworth folk have long memories!'

'Jimmy!' Philippa was stung to exasperation. 'I'd have though better of you!'

'Sorry I'm such a disappointment, then.' He turned away from her. 'You make sure Alex Penfold don't disappoint you as well. If he does, you'll know where to come.'

He slouched out of the porch with his shoulders hunched. Philippa watched him go with a feeling of dismay. She was staring after him when Alex touched her on the shoulder.

'Let him go!' he said. 'He ruined our walk yesterday. Don't let him spoil today as well.'

Still smarting from her encounter with Jimmy she snapped at Alex.

'That wasn't his fault. What's so special about today, anyway?'

'Mother would like you and your

70

father to join us for Sunday lunch. Your father said he'd like to come if it's all right with you.'

Philippa felt out manoeuvred. She looked for her father and saw he was still talking to Lizzie.

'Well,' she said, none too graciously, 'if he wants to . . .'

'Good! Then shall we go? They can follow on.' Alex caught his mother's eye and indicated that he and Philippa were leaving. 'I wanted a quiet word with you, anyway,' he said as they left the church. 'It's about this dinner. Mother and Peggy think they can cope with it between them so I'd like to fix it for next Saturday if you can manage then.'

'Yes. I think Saturday's OK.'

As they walked down the hill from the church he began asking about her music, wanting to know what had made her take up the harp in the first place.

'I started on the piano,' she said, 'like most kids,' and explained that it was when she was at school in Exeter and the student orchestra needed a harpist that she was persuaded to try the instrument. 'I loved it straightaway,' she said. 'I felt — I don't know — as if we belonged together.'

'I can tell that from watching you play.' He moved closer and took her arm. 'It's instinctive, isn't it, knowing where you belong? It's the way I feel about you.'

'But people are different!' she objected. 'You can't belong to somebody, not completely!'

'I'd have to share you with your harp, is that what you're trying to say?'

'I was talking generally, Alex!'

'All the same, you wouldn't want to give it up.'

'Of course not!'

'As long as I know where I stand.'

They were nearing the centre of the village and Philippa stopped abruptly.

'Look, Alex!' she said. 'As far as I'm concerned you don't really stand anywhere. I'm not ready for this and I don't want it. You're pushing things, just as you are with the men. Go easy, can't you? What's all the rush?'

'The rush is because I don't want to lose you now I've found you. I don't want to lose any of it because I've waited for so long. Can't you understand?'

'But the estate won't go away! Nor will I unless I get offered a marvellous job somewhere.'

'That's what worries me. You're too good, Philippa.'

'Oh, thanks very much!' she flashed back at him. 'You'd rather I wasn't so good, is that it? You'd like me to be on hand all the time, just playing at the odd concert or for your business friends whenever you wanted me to!'

'No!' She caught a glint of anger in his eyes. 'I can see you want to be a success.'

'Can you? Can you really, Alex?'

'Of course. You're very talented. You're thinking about your career.

That's only natural. So whatever happens between us, I promise I'd never stand in your way.'

'Don't worry! I wouldn't let you!' She looked past him up the hill. 'They're catching us up. Shall we wait for them?'

'No. When we get to the manor I'd like you to choose which room you want to play in next Saturday. The dining-room or the library, I thought.'

They began walking again. Her heart was pounding. But at least I've told him, she thought. He knows now he can't just sweep into my life and expect to change it completely. She was astonished at her own boldness and by the way he had apparently accepted her conditions.

They walked on in silence until they turned into the lane leading to the manor. Then he surprised her again by saying, 'I'm sorry if I've been rushing you, Philippa. I'll back off a little, if you'd rather.'

'I wish you would. Sarah and I have

a couple of recitals at a festival in Bristol the week after next so I'm going to be busy. Can't we just leave it that I'll see you next week-end at the dinner for your friends?'

'If you insist.'

He sounded disappointed but she hardened her heart. I must have breathing space from him, she thought, and time to discover what I really feel!

She chose the library to play in rather than the dining-room which seemed too formal with its long, polished table, its stiff-backed dining chairs and gleaming candelabra. The library was more intimate.

The guests could sit around in comfortable armchairs and she could set up her harp in the window recess. She had already chosen what she intended to play, pieces by Handel, Mozart and William Boyce which were more or less in period.

'As long as it's something to give a feeling of the manor's history,' Alex said. 'You and Mother can chat to the ladies afterwards while we men get down to business.'

'You're going to make good use of me!'

'It could be valuable for you as well! These people have a lot of influence.'

'Which is why you cultivate them?'

'Of course.' He smiled at her evident score. 'But I like them as well. It would be harder if I didn't. Oh, come oh, Philippa! You must do much the same in the music world. It's whom you know these days.'

'Is it? I always thought it was what you could do!'

'That as well! But don't let's argue. Let's go and see how Peggy Tucker's getting on with lunch.'

Peggy had cooked them spring lamb with rosemary and followed that with fresh strawberries and clotted cream. They ate in the breakfast room as there were only four of them and took their coffee outside on the patio afterwards.

It was on the sunny side of the house

and Arthur Penfold had surrounded it with beds of roses which filled the air with perfume.

They sat there for a long time, Philippa listening with interest as her father and Lizzie reminisced about life in the village when they were young.

Then Alex, who was beginning to show signs of restlessness, suddenly jumped up and said he had a proposition to put to Martin. He wanted to take him down to the farm to discuss it.

'We won't be long,' he told Philippa. 'It'll give you and Mother a chance to get to know one another.'

Philippa raised her eyebrows as he disappeared with her father.

'Does he always order people about like this?' she asked Lizzie.

'He tries to. You just have to stand up to him!' Lizzie sighed. 'I'm afraid he's in too much of a hurry these days. His father died convinced he didn't get a fair deal out of life so Alex is determined to take all he can while he can.'

'I've noticed!'

Lizzie put a hand over one of Philippa's.

'Be patient with him! He thinks a lot of you. You could be good for him.'

'I hardly know him, Mrs Penfold!'

'Does that matter? You can live with people for years and never get to know them. I found that out.' She gave Philippa's hand a squeeze. 'But take no notice of me! We make our choices for better or worse and you won't make yours until you're ready.' She smiled. 'It's such a lovely day, Philippa! We don't have to wait here because Alex told us to! Let's stroll down to the farm and meet them.'

The sound of raised voices was audible even before Lizzie and Philippa reached the farmhouse. When they rounded the corner of the barn they saw that Alex was engaged in a heated argument with Jeff and Jimmy Laramy. Martin was standing a little apart from them, looking embarrassed. When he caught sight of Philippa, he walked over to her and Lizzie.

'What's going on?' Philippa asked in consternation.

'Some row about the sheep,' Martin muttered. 'Jeff's hired his usual gang for the shearing next month and Alex says he should have been consulted. He reckons the bill he's just had for hay and silage is much too high and that Jeff must be taking a back-hander for himself.'

'Oh, no!'

'Then Jeff said Arthur Penfold always trusted him to see to the general running of the farm and that Alex doesn't know the first thing about it. Now they're arguing about what's to go to market when the sales start in the autumn. Jeff wants to keep his winter stock of Closewools but Alex is all for getting rid of them and buying in Exmoor Horns. He said he'll look for a new manager if Jeff won't co-operate.'

'And get rid of the Laramys?'

'Not if I can help it!' Lizzie

declared. To Philippa's astonishment she marched over to the group of men. 'Now then, Jeff Laramy,' she demanded, 'what's all this about? Still making trouble, like you did at school?'

'Keep out of this, Mother!' Alex snapped. 'The estate's my affair.'

'But you're still mine and you seem to be out-numbered here. Whatever this is about won't be solved by shouting so you'd best all calm down and come up to the house to discuss it!'

'You give the orders now, then!' Jeff Laramy sneered. 'Come up in the world, haven't you, Lizzie Ash?'

'Don't you speak to my mother like that!' Alex raged.

'Take no notice!' Lizzie said. 'He always was a bully.'

'Bully, was I?' Jeff's eyes narrowed. 'And what were you, then? I don't suppose you've told him you never knew who his father was!'

There was a moment's shocked silence and Philippa saw Alex's face

80

whiten. Then he flew at Jeff and punched him hard on the shoulder, making him stagger. Jimmy gave a shout of indignation and hit out at Alex. Soon the two young men were pummelling one another.

'Oh! Stop them!' Lizzie screamed.

Martin rushed over to intervene while Philippa watched appalled, fearful for her father.

'Stop it!' she cried. 'You're no better than savages.'

Then Jeff took a hand as well and he and Martin between them dragged Jimmy and Alex apart, leaving them glaring at one another, breathless.

'That's it, then!' Alex panted. 'I'll give you two a month to leave the farm! Both of you! Just clear out!'

'No!' Lizzie cried. 'We must talk it over!'

'There's nothing to talk about!' Alex swung away from them all and began striding back to the manor, ignoring his mother and the others who stood stunned and speechless.

Then Lizzie found her voice.

'Well, you've done it now, Jeff Laramy! You always were a big mouth!'

Her lips were trembling as she began following Alex back to the house. She stumbled a little and Martin hurried after her and took her arm.

'Why?' Philippa demanded of Jeff Laramy. 'It was all so long ago. Why did you have to hurt her like that?'

'She riled me,' he muttered. 'And that son of hers wants to change everything.'

'Well, you haven't helped yourself today, have you? Or the estate! Will he really make you leave the farm?'

'He'll have to get the bailiffs in before we'll budge! Isn't that so, Jimmy?'

Philippa looked at Jimmy who shook his head in bewilderment.

'I never thought it'd come to this,' he said. 'Perhaps you or your dad could speak for us, Philippa, as you get on with him so well.'

'Oh, Jimmy!' Philippa said. 'He'd

never listen to me! It's between the Laramys and the Penfolds now and you'll just have to sort it out yourself.'

At that moment she didn't even want to help them. She was remembering the shock in Alex's face when Jeff Laramy made his accusation and the guilt in Lizzie's eyes before she hurried after her son.

If anybody needs help it's Alex, she thought and wished she could go to him and put her arms round him to comfort him. But she knew it was too soon for that. Alex's pride would not let him accept pity and he would need time to come to an understanding with his mother.

'I'm sorry,' she said to the Laramys. 'I hope he changes his mind for all your sakes. But you must see, I can't do anything about it.'

She left them then and walked miserably back to the cottage on her own, wondering what was happening in the manor.

It was a long time before Martin

came home and she had the kettle on for tea when he appeared.

'Well?' she asked anxiously. 'What happened?'

Martin sank gratefully into his favourite armchair.

'Nothing much. Alex didn't come back to the house. We spotted him charging off into the woods. I suppose he had to give vent to his feelings.'

'I'm not surprised after what Jeff said.'

'It was rough on Lizzie, too. She was pretty upset but she's putting a brave face on it. She thinks she might be able to persuade Alex to change his mind about the Laramys but I doubt it.'

'So do I.' Philippa hesitated. 'Was there any truth in Jeff's story?'

'Well, folk always reckoned Lizzie was too free with both the Penfold brothers but who can tell? They're dead and she's the only one who knows. She'll stick to her own version but Alex will never be quite sure after this.'

'So how well did you know Lizzie, Dad?'

'I told you — we were at school together.'

Philippa sensed her father clam up so she did not press the point. Instead she asked, 'What did Alex want to discuss with you this afternoon?'

'We didn't get far before the bust-up with Laramys. But he's thinking about turning some of his redundant barns into craft workshops and wondered if I'd like to move into one.'

'Oh! Are you interested?' Philippa asked eagerly.

'I might be if the business expands. But I'm not too keen on being on show. That's what he wants — craftsmen at work while his visitors watch. Part of his theme park.'

'As long as he doesn't expect you to dress up!'

They both laughed and some of the gloom of the afternoon lifted. But Philippa could not dismiss Alex from her mind. He invaded her dreams that night. She was running from him in the woods, and this time, when he swept her up into his arms, she laughed and welcomed him gladly. Then the woods suddenly became dark and threatening, closing in over their heads. She awoke with a cry, her heart pounding.

It was a long time before she could get to sleep again and she was heavy-eyed the next morning, weighed down by a feeling of foreboding.

6

By the next day, it was all over the village that Alex Penfold had given the Laramys notice to quit the manor farm. Jeff and Jimmy had drowned their sorrows in the Penworth Arms on Sunday evening and, as a result, local opinion was all on their side.

Nobody believed it would come to the Laramys actually leaving, not over a management dispute which was all they had admitted to. Only Martin and Philippa knew there was more to it than that and were afraid Alex was unlikely to change his mind.

'But he can't find a new farm manager in a hurry,' Martin said at breakfast on Monday morning. 'He'll have to let the Laramys stay until he finds a replacement for Jeff.'

Philippa sighed. 'He's very determined. He'll ask around and there's a lot of unemployment in farming. I just wish there was something we could do but there isn't, is there?'

'No.' Martin stood up to go. 'Best to keep out of it, Pippa. I'm off to the workshop. Can't sit here all day.'

Left to herself, Philippa cleared away the breakfast things, pulled her harp from its place in the alcove and began to play. But the old magic was missing and her harp failed to sing to her the way it usually did. She had to see Alex.

She slipped out of the cottage without telling Martin where she was going and hurried down the hill. If I could just make Alex understand he's going about it all the wrong way, she thought. His mother must know that because she knows Penworth. Perhaps, between us, we could influence him.

But although she had set out so boldly, she approached the manor with trepidation. After all, she had told Alex she did not want to see him until Saturday. So how would he receive her, knowing she had witnessed the bitter row between himself and the Laramys?

When she tugged on the heavy door pull and waited, she felt her heart quickening at the thought of having to face him. Why does he have such an effect on me, she wondered. Why do I feel I have to help him when he makes most of his troubles for himself? Impossible man! Why do I care so much?

She could no longer deny that she did care and her heart leaped alarmingly when the old oak door swung open. It was Peggy Tucker who had answered.

'Oh, it's you, Miss Southcott,' she said. 'Are you expected?'

'Well, no. But — is Mr Penfold in?'

'He's in but he said he wasn't to be disturbed. He's very busy in his study.'

'I see. And Mrs Penfold?'

'She's off in the car, fetching all sorts of fancy stuff from South Molton.'

Peggy sniffed. 'They've got this dinner on Saturday. Putting on the grand.'

'I know. Actually — ' Philippa sought for an excuse to see Alex. 'It's about the dinner I want to see Mr Penfold.'

'Oh, of course! You're playing at it. Well, I don't know anything about that.'

'Then perhaps you could ask Mr Penfold if he could spare a few minutes.'

'I suppose I could try. You'd best come in, then.'

She left Philippa waiting in the outer hall while she went to speak to Alex. His study was in the depths of the house and it seemed an age before Peggy returned. When she did there was a knowing smirk on her face.

'He says as it's you, you can come through. But he can't give you more than ten minutes.'

Philippa's colour was high as she followed Peggy. She had come because she was sorry for Alex and wanted to help him. Now she felt furious at being treated like a salesman or one of his farm workers and she was not inclined to smile when he rose to greet her.

'Philippa!' he said. 'This is a surprise. I hope you haven't come to tell me you can't play on Saturday.'

'No. I always honour my engagements.'

'Good. Thanks, Peggy. Shut the door when you go out.' He turned to Philippa. 'Won't you sit down? There's nothing wrong, is there?'

'Wrong?' His calm formality so irritated her she stayed on her feet, the better to confront him. 'How can you ask that after yesterday? Everything's wrong, Alex! The village is up in arms because of the way you treated the Laramys!'

'Was I supposed to stand by when Jeff Laramy insulted my mother?'

'No! But if you hadn't worked him up to it he'd never have said what he did!'

'Wouldn't he? He'd said plenty in the village before that. It wasn't an isolated incident, Philippa. He and people like him are making life very uncomfortable for my mother, just as they did years ago.'

'Oh!' Philippa sat down. 'I didn't know that. All the same, it's very hard on them to be turned out after all the years their family's worked on the estate. Perhaps you didn't know that Jeff's father was farm manager before him. Surely you could take that into account?'

'Is this what you've come to say?'

'Yes. Well — partly. Yesterday, I felt so sorry for you. You were hurt, I could see that. But I didn't know what to do. I wanted to help but you just went.'

'I had to be alone!' he said harshly.

'Of course. But afterwards . . . '

'I needed you!' he said. 'I needed you so badly I went to the hermitage and willed you to come. Why didn't you come to me?'

'I wanted to but I wasn't sure. I was upset because of the Laramys. I was torn in two, Alex.'

'And you still are, aren't you?'

'Yes,' she admitted and looked away so that she couldn't see the disappointment in his eyes. For a moment neither of them spoke. Then Alex said, 'My mother's like you. She thinks I've been too hard.'

'So?' Philippa turned back to him eagerly.

'I'm still considering what to do. I may leave the Laramys at the farm but bring in a new stockman, somebody who'll be more interested in introducing the old breeds. I've an empty cottage he could have so there wouldn't be a problem about accommodation.'

'I see.'

'That's why I'm busy this morning. I'm ringing round to find out who's available. But I shan't tell the Laramys yet. I want an apology from them first so they can stew in their own juice for a bit. That won't do them any harm.'

'No.' Philippa felt a rush of relief. 'It would be marvellous if you could let them stay on!'

'You're not to tell them, Philippa!'

'Oh, I won't. But I'm so glad!' She stood up to go. 'I won't hinder you any longer, then, as you're so busy.'

He got up, too, and came from behind his desk to take her hands in his His arms went round her and when their mouths met she felt such a shudder of desire she closed her eyes and clung to him helplessly. It was as if she belonged in his arms and had no strength of will to draw away. When at last he let her go she knew she was already lost.

'Goodbye, Philippa,' he said roughly. 'I'll see you on Saturday. That's what we decided, wasn't it?'

'Yes. Seven thirty, isn't it?'

'Oh, come earlier and meet my guests. You'll like them.'

'Will I?' She smiled tremulously. 'Thanks, anyway, for everything, Alex.'

'Don't thank me too soon!' he warned. 'A lot depends on your friends, the Laramys. I still want that apology. It's not for me. It's for my mother.'

'Can I tell them that, at least?'

'Please yourself.' He opened the study door for her. 'You can find your own way out, can't you?'

She felt his eyes on her as she walked along the corridor but when she looked back he had gone and his study door was firmly shut.

Upon an impulse she headed towards the woods. The path through them to the farm was a longer way round but she did not want anyone from the house to see where she was going.

There was nobody about in the farmyard when she reached it and no answer to her call at the back door of the farm house. She supposed Mrs Laramy must be in the village and the men at work somewhere.

She could hear the distant hum of a machine and followed the sound until she caught sight of Jeff Laramy on the four-wheeled motorbike he used for driving up the steep fields of the estate. His black and white Welsh collie was circling round him and the top pastures were full of sheep so he had evidently been doing the rounds of his stock.

She made her way along the farm track, opened the five-bar gate and began the climb through the damp grass towards him. His dog raced towards her and Jeff switched off his motor and waited for her to reach him.

'What be you doing up this way?' he growled. 'Looking for Jimmy, are you?'

'No.' She reached down to smooth the sleek head of the collie fussing around her. 'I wanted a word with you.'

'Oh! Honoured, I'm sure!'

She ignored his sarcasm and went straight to the point.

'What are you going to do about Mrs Penfold, Jeff?'

'Lizzie Ash? What should I do about her?'

'Don't you think you owe her an apology?'

'Why? I only said what everybody knows.'

'You said what too many people are gossiping about. The village gave her a bad time once. But that was years ago and best forgotten. I know you don't see eye to eye with Alex but there was no need to be so cruel to his mother. Why don't you make the first move, Jeff, and tell her you're sorry?'

'What's in it for you, then? Why are you so interested?'

'I just don't like seeing people hurt.'

'Then him down there in the manor should have thought of that before he chucked us out of the farm!'

'You haven't gone yet!'

'No. And we're not going! He's the one who ought to apologise. Treated us like dirt, he did.'

'Look, Jeff!' Philippa softened her approach. 'I know there's fault on both sides. I'm not asking you to bow down to Alex — just — well, to show willing and try to make things a bit easier for Lizzie. You used to know her, after all.'

'Oh, yes!' He laughed unpleasantly.

'We all knew Lizzie! That was her trouble. You ask your old man! So it's no use her coming back here trying to play the lady!'

'That's a dreadful thing to say!'

'Well, what did you expect?' He switched on his motor again. 'You'd best watch out, too, Philippa! He may be sweet talking you now but he's a Penfold. And there'll be plenty of Lizzie in him as well, you mark my words!'

'So you won't say you're sorry?' Philippa shouted as he began to move off.

'It takes two to mend a quarrel,' he shouted back. 'You tell Lizzie Ash that from me, if you ever get the chance!'

What did he mean, Philippa wondered as she watched him roar away. Was there an earlier quarrel between him and Alex's mother none of us know about?

She felt out of her depth and wished she had not come. Perhaps she should have approached Jimmy instead. But Jimmy had always been under his father's thumb which was one reason her friendship with him had not developed into anything deeper.

She walked home, feeling depressed. As she reached the cottage, she heard the phone ringing. It was Sarah suggesting it was time they got together to rehearse for the Bristol Arts Festival.

She said they had been asked to give another recital at a festival in Plymouth the following month and that an orchestra they ought to apply for was being got together to accompany a massed choir performance.

Philippa knew she should be feeling as excited as her friend but when she replaced the receiver she realised she was maybe only making these plans to fill in time before she could see Alex again.

Yet she practised hard all week until the Friday evening when her father came home from the Penworth Arms with disturbing news. Alex had been interviewing for a new stockman and had shown the most likely applicant around the estate that afternoon.

'Jeff Laramy's absolutely furious!' Martin said. 'He wouldn't do the rounds with them or co-operate at all. Mrs Laramy didn't even offer them a cup of tea.'

Philippa was dismayed.

'What are they going to do?'

'They're trying to stir up the village — get up a petition, or something. There's going to be trouble, I fear.'

'If only Jeff would apologise! I'm sure that's all it would take.'

Her father shook his head.

'There's no reasoning with him. He says he'll stay on at the farm whatever happens. As for Jimmy, he just goes around looking miserable, poor lad.'

She made up her mind to find Jimmy and get him to persuade his father to take a softer line with Alex. It was their only hope.

The next morning she went along to Arthur Penfold's gardens, but Jimmy was not there and the lad who helped him with the heavy work told her that he and Jeff were both in the village, collecting signatures for their petition.

'And there's going to be fine fun later on,' he said and chuckled. 'Seems there's a do at the manor tonight so we're all going along there to demonstrate.'

'You can't do that!' Philippa cried. 'Did Jimmy put you up to it?'

'Well, it's like him and his dad said, it's them getting it now but it'll be the rest of us soon. So us be all going tonight.'

I must stop them, she thought. She hurried back to the village only to discover that Jeff and Jimmy had called at the cottage with their petition some time earlier.

'You didn't sign it?' she asked her father anxiously.

'No,' Martin said. 'I told them they were going the wrong way about it. But they'd collected a lot of signatures and said they're going to deliver the petition tonight.'

'I know. The idiots have persuaded the rest of the men to go along with them to demonstrate. Alex has all these people coming so he'll be furious. How can we stop them?'

'Leave it, Pippa! Don't get involved!'

'But I'm involved already! Don't you see? I'll be there tonight so I'll be in the thick of it!'

7

To Philippa's dismay, Alex was not at the manor when she arrived so Peggy Tucker showed her into the morning-room. Lizzie had her feet up and seemed genuinely pleased to see her.

'Bring us in some tea, Peggy,' she said.

'Where's Alex?' Philippa asked.

'Gone to Exeter to meet some of his friends from the London train. The others are driving down. There's nothing wrong, is there?'

'I'm afraid there could be.' Philippa explained about the Laramy's petition and the demonstration planned for that evening.

Lizzie shook her head wearily. 'It needn't have come to this! It could all have been settled last Sunday if he'd listened to me.'

'I think he wants Jeff to apologise.'

'Then he'll wait for ever! Jeff was always a hard man.'

'I had a word with him on Monday.'

'With Jeff?' Lizzie looked up with interest. 'What did he say?'

'He said to tell you it takes two to mend a quarrel.'

She saw Lizzie flinch.

'To tell me? You're sure that's what he said?'

'Quite sure.'

'Some people never forget,' she said. 'D'you think I should talk to him?'

'Not if it upsets you.'

Lizzie was silent, for a moment. Then she said, 'When you're young, you're selfish. You don't realise how easily people get hurt.'

Philippa waited, expecting more. But just as it seemed Lizzie was about to confide in her, Peggy came in with their tea and the moment passed.

Their conversation after that touched on nothing deeper than the menu for that night's dinner and the music Philippa had chosen to play. But when she rose to go, Lizzie caught hold of her hand and held it tightly.

'Don't worry about tonight!' she said. 'I'll warn Alex but I'm sure nothing will happen. Jeff Laramy's all talk. Just come and enjoy yourself! Alex is looking forward to having you here and I know you'll do him proud.'

Philippa dressed with particular care for the evening, putting on the same gown she had worn for the recital in the church but adding a lacy stole that had been her mother's.

'You're looking very pretty tonight, Pippa,' her father said when she went downstairs. 'Isn't that your mother's stole?'

'Yes. I thought it would go with this dress.'

'She'd like that. She'd be as proud of you as I am. You've grown up a lot since you left college.'

Or since I met Alex, Philippa wondered, uneasily.

'It must be all these concerts!' she said. 'I'm a professional now! Will you give me a hand with my harp before I go?'

She drove herself to the manor, arriving just before seven. When she parked in the forecourt she saw that Alex's car was already there, together with two strange cars. They're all here then, she thought. She slipped from the driver's seat and was about to start unloading her harp when the door of the manor burst open and Alex came running down the stone steps towards her.

'Leave that!' he cried. 'I'll lift it out. I've been watching for you from the morning-room window. Why didn't you come earlier? I needed you to help with all the women!'

'How many are there?'

'Only four,' he admitted. 'But I run out of things to say to them.'

'What you mean is, you only want to talk business with their husbands!'

He grinned.

'Come on in and meet everybody! I've been telling them all about you.'

He seemed his usual confident self and was looking so handsome in his dinner suit her heart turned over.

'Did your mother tell you I was here this afternoon?' she asked.

'This afternoon?' He frowned. 'Oh, yes — some nonsense about the Laramys and a demonstration. I rang the farm and warned them off. We shouldn't have any trouble.' He wheeled the harp on its trolley to the bottom of the entrance steps and paused. 'Wait here a minute, Philippa! I'll have to get somebody to help carry it in. Don't want to damage it.'

He disappeared inside, leaving Philippa perplexed. He didn't seem at all worried that the Laramys might ruin his evening. Did he really suppose a phone call was enough to make Jeff call off his demonstration?

When Alex reappeared he had a stocky, middle-aged man with him whom he introduced as Tony. Between them they carried the harp up the steps and into the entrance hall. Philippa followed with her music and her stand, hearing the distant sound of voices and laughter coming from the morning-room.

'May as well wheel it straight through to the library,' Alex said to Tony. 'Thanks, old man. We can manage now. Come with me, Philippa, and show me where you want it.'

Together they trundled the harp into the library and set it up in the window recess. Alex pulled the red velvet curtains behind it and found a high-backed chair for Philippa.

'Sit there and let me judge the effect!' he said and stood back, narrowing his eyes as she posed for him. 'Ah, yes! Very romantic.'

'But I'm not in period!' she teased. 'Still, the music will be.'

'What matters most is that you're here!' He moved towards her and took her hand, drawing her to her feet. 'I miss you when you're not around.'

'Do you?' The look in his eyes made her heart race.

'You know I do. I've kept away because you asked me to but it's been difficult.' He searched her face. 'Have you missed me?'

'I've been too busy,' she lied.

'I've been busy as well but it hasn't helped! So how long do we have to keep this up?'

'I've two recitals next week and a couple more soon.'

'That's only one part of your life, Philippa! Can't you let me share some of the rest of it? Don't keep shutting me out, my darling!'

His arms tightened round her and suddenly they were clinging to one another in a kind of desperation. When their mouths met it was with a passion that frightened her. When he finally let her go her breath was coming fast and she stared at him, wide-eyed.

'I'm still not sure how I feel,' she stammered nervously.

'You've just shown me how you feel!'

'But I don't really know you, Alex.

We disagree so often. And you're so hard-hearted sometimes. I mean, this business with the Laramys . . .'

'So it's back to them, is it?'

'You don't understand how much the farm means to them! Then there's the estate. You go blindly on, riding roughshod over everybody.'

She saw him turn away, a bleak look on his face.

'So that's it!' he said flatly. 'You think I'm rushing even you — that I wouldn't give you a life of your own.'

'I think you'd intend giving me a life of my own. I'm not sure if you'd managed to if it ever came to the point.'

He turned back to her then and gripped her hands fiercely.

'I love you, Philippa. I'd never do anything to hurt you.'

She smiled a little sadly.

'I know you wouldn't, not deliberately. I just need more time. Don't you see?'

His eyes smouldered. 'No! I don't

see. But I can go on waiting if I must! But I don't want to have to wait for too long, Philippa!' He took her arm. 'At least you're my partner tonight and I'm proud of you. So let's join the guests! I want to introduce you to everybody.'

He would have led her out of the library but she held back.

'Alex — before we go — don't underestimate the Laramys! They've been around the village getting signatures to their petition and there's a lot of local feeling on their side. They could still show up tonight.'

'If they do, they'll meet more than they've bargained for. I've rung the police. The Laramys know it would only take one call from me to get them here.'

With his hand under her elbow he propelled her through the doorway. Eight pairs of eyes turned towards them when they entered the morning-room for there were four couples. The men were wearing formal dinner suits like Alex and the women were stylishly coiffured and all, except one, expensively-dressed in short cocktail dresses which made Philippa feel out of place in her long one. They looked older than Alex apart from one pair who proved to be American when Philippa was introduced to them.

The wife was a vivacious strawberry blonde, flamboyant in a glittering, trouser suit. She welcomed Philippa with open arms.

'A harpist!' she exclaimed. 'Ever since I was a little girl, I've wanted to play the harp! Isn't that so, Lloyd?' she appealed to her husband. 'Tell me, Philippa, does it take a long time to learn?'

Alex chuckled as he poured Philippa a drink.

'It sounds as if you and Myrtle will have plenty to talk about!'

'We certainly will!' Myrtle said. 'I've always been interested in music but somehow I've never had the time to take it up.'

She monopolised Philippa from then on and even contrived to sit opposite her at dinner so that she could continue their conversation.

Peggy Tucker served them but Lizzie remained hidden in the kitchen, putting the finishing touches to each dish before it arrived.

The wine kept the conversation flowing and, despite her misgivings, Philippa began to enjoy herself. Alex was an exuberant host and obviously delighted with the way things were going until the man called Tony suddenly asked him how far he had got with his plan to bring back some of the older breeds of sheep and cattle to the farm. Philippa saw Alex frown.

'It's going ahead,' he said. 'Of course, we can't do much until the sales start in the autumn.'

'I just wondered how your manager's taking it,' Tony said. 'Rumour has it they don't like changes down in this neck of the woods.'

'They'll do what they're told,' Alex said shortly.

Philippa saw Tony raise his eyebrows

and glance at one of the other men. When the meal was over and they all began to leave the table, she noticed the two of them hanging back to have a word with one another. Were they having doubts about investing in Alex's plans for the estate?

He had gone to the kitchen to fetch his mother so that she could be congratulated on the meal.

'The next time you come,' Lizzie told his guests, 'we'll be able to offer you a real eighteenth-century banquet. So do tell all your friends, won't you?'

There was a murmur of interest and approval and Alex beamed at his mother. He insisted she should join them in the library for the music and once that began, Philippa was too engrossed to worry about Tony or what the Laramys might do.

In the intimacy of the library her harp resounded bell-like and she smiled as she played, aware of Alex watching her and wondering if he realised she was playing mostly for him. When the applause came she knew she had succeeded in pleasing her audience. Only Tony looked morose as he clapped but Myrtle was ecstatic in her praise.

'While you were playing, Philippa,' she said, 'I imagined this room full of eighteenth-century ladies and gentlemen in their wigs and courtly costumes! And if I could ever learn to play like that, I guess I'd be in Heaven!'

Everybody laughed and when Philippa caught Alex's approving eye she knew she had created the atmosphere he wanted. He thanked her and suggested that she and Lizzie should take the ladies back to the morning-room while the men got down to business.

They were preparing to go when Peggy Tucker came hurrying in and muttered something to Lizzie who beckoned to Alex. The three of them stood huddled in consultation for a minute or two while the rest of the company became gradually silent, sensing that something was wrong.

Although Alex was smiling when he turned towards them again, Philippa could tell he was tense.

'Will you stay where you are for a moment, ladies?' he asked. 'I've something to attend to. Won't take long.'

He went out with Peggy and Lizzie. Philippa hurried after them.

'What is it?' she asked him. 'What's happened?'

'It's the Laramys. They've got a mob with them outside the morning-room. I'm going to ring the police.'

'No!' Lizzie cried. 'Not until you've spoken to them!'

'Why should I waste time talking to those idiots?'

'Because you need them, Alex!'

'They're doing this deliberately,' he raged. 'They know we've guests!'

'Oh, go and talk to them, Alex!' Philippa pleaded. 'Give them a chance!'

'You as well?' He glared at them both. 'You're as soft as one another!'

'Not soft!' Lizzie said. 'Just sensible!

116

We know these people.'

'I'd have thought you've known them only too well!'

'Yes.' Lizzie turned away from him. 'So if you won't speak to them, I must!'

She began making for the other hall and Alex ran after her.

'Don't be a fool, Mother! Let me deal with this!'

Philippa ran to the morning-room and looked out. It was still light and she could see Jeff and Jimmy Laramy with the other men from the estate, a few village lads and several of their drinking companions from the Penworth Arms.

Some of them were carrying buckets which they were banging with sticks. The gardener's boy and another lad were waving banners about and grinning.

She heard excited voices behind her and turned to see Alex's guests coming into the morning-room. They all crowded round the window exclaiming until there came a sharp crack as a stone hit it.

'Stand back!' Tony cried. 'There's a bunch of madmen out there!'

Another stone flew from the crowd, cracking a corner of the window and making the women shriek. Then there was fresh commotion outside as Lizzie appeared, running towards Jeff Laramy with Alex close behind her. He caught at her arm and made her stumble but she shook him off and started gesticulating and saying something to Jeff.

Nobody saw who threw the next stone. Philippa was sure it was not meant for Lizzie, but it caught her on the side of her face and she staggered and fell. The banging stopped abruptly. All the men backed away except Jeff who went down on his knees beside Lizzie to lift her up. But Alex pushed him roughly aside. Philippa was already running out on to the forecourt. She met Alex, carrying Lizzie in.

'Ring the police!' he ordered.

'No!' Lizzie pleaded.

'Do it, Philippa!' Alex's eyes were

blazing and his face was grim when she hesitated. 'Now!' he commanded. 'And ring the doctor!'

He carried Lizzie into the entrance hall where his guests stood aghast. He pushed his way through them and strode determinedly up the main staircase.

Myrtle caught at Philippa's arm.

'What's going on?' she asked. 'Poor Mrs Penfold! Is she badly hurt?'

'I hope not. Don't worry! It's just a bit of local bother. Nothing serious.'

Philippa hurried on towards the study where she could telephone without being overheard. As she passed Tony she heard him mutter to the man he had been talking to earlier.

'So it's true! He is having trouble. Better think twice about putting money in.'

Philippa knew what that meant and feared for Alex and the Laramys. He would be even more furious with them if he lost his backers. She did not want to phone the police but dared not defy him. In any case, damage had been done and Lizzie had been hurt. The police would have to be told.

Once in the study she picked up the receiver reluctantly and made the call. Then she phoned the local doctor. After that she went upstairs by the back way to find Alex and see how Lizzie was faring.

8

Alex was in his mother's bedroom and Lizzie was lying propped up on her bed with Peggy Tucker bathing the cut on her face.

'Can I do anything?' Philippa asked.

'You'd be more use downstairs, taking care of my guests!' Alex said roughly. 'What's happening? Has the mob gone?'

'I don't know. I came up by the back way.'

'Fools!' Alex grated. 'I should have sorted them out long before this!'

Lizzie touched his hand.

'Why don't you go down? Philippa can stay with me. And Peggy's here.'

'I suppose I ought to be there when the police arrive. Did you see who was with the Laramys, Philippa? They weren't all from the estate.'

'There were two or three village lads.

I only know them by sight. And a few men I've seen in the pub.'

'The police will need names.' He rounded on Peggy. 'So what about you? You must know them all.'

Peggy's eyes flickered.

'Oh, I didn't see anything, Mr Penfold! I came straight for you and kept out of it. I didn't want any trouble.'

Alex gave a harsh laugh. 'Of course, you'll all cover up for one another. So who started throwing stones? Did you see that, Philippa?'

She shook her head.

'I'm sure it wasn't Jimmy or Jeff. The stones came from the back of the crowd.'

'And they weren't meant for me,' Lizzie said wearily. 'I've told you that. I just got in the way.'

'I can't think what possessed you!' Alex looked down at his mother with a mixture of irritation and concern.

She turned her face away and Philippa saw the same pain in her eyes that had been there that afternoon. So what were you trying to do, Lizzie, she wondered. Appeal to Jeff? Settle your own private quarrel?

She looked at Alex who seemed torn between staying with his mother and attending to matters downstairs.

'I'll go down if you'd rather stay here,' she offered. 'I could let you know when the police arrive.'

'No. I'd better go down. They'll be wondering what's happening.' He bent over Lizzie to kiss her cheek. 'Sure you'll be all right?'

'Of course.' Lizzie smiled wanly. 'And take Philippa with you! I don't need two people to look after me.'

Philippa caught a flash of relief in Alex's eyes as he turned to her.

'I could do with you to keep the ladies happy,' he said.

Once they were outside Lizzie's room, he muttered, 'What have they been saying downstairs?'

'Not much. It was all so sudden.'

I don't think I'll tell him what I

overheard, she decided, because he'll find out soon enough.

'I should have listened to you.' he said. 'And taken the Laramys seriously.'

'There's still time to do that.'

They had reached the top of the main staircase and he stopped abruptly.

'You're not still on their side? Not after tonight?'

'No more than I'm on yours! Alex, it must be settled, this stupid quarrel. It's tearing the estate and the village apart. You didn't even accept their petition.'

'How could I? They didn't give me a chance!'

'No.' She touched his arm contritely. 'I'm sorry. I'm afraid they've ruined your evening.'

'As long as they haven't ruined more than that! Come on! We'd better try to smooth things over with our guests. I've planned a tour of the estate for tomorrow. God knows if that will be possible now.'

The guests were still in the morning-room, the men conferring in a huddle at one corner of it and the women chatting nervously in another. All talking ceased when Alex and Philippa came in.

Alex moved to the window.

'I see they've gone,' he said. 'Sorry about all that. Just a little local trouble.'

'But how is poor Mrs Penfold?' Myrtle asked in concern.

'She's being looked after and she's not badly hurt. The doctor's on his way.'

'And the police?' Tony asked. 'You've called them, I hope. I've never seen such a disgraceful exhibition!' He approached Alex with a paper in his hand. 'Here! You'd better have this.'

'What is it?'

'It looks like a petition. One of your fellows had the nerve to come up to the door with it so I took it in. It's collected a lot of signatures for a little local trouble!'

Alex's lips tightened as he scrunched

the paper between his fingers.

'I'll take a look at it later.'

There was an awkward pause.

Myrtle broke it by rushing in with, 'Philippa, do come and join us! You must have a word with Janey! She has a cousin who's on the board of one of the big London orchestras. I'm sure she'd introduce you to him if you wanted.'

Philippa was drawn reluctantly towards the women, leaving Alex alone. She glanced back at him and saw him straighten his shoulders before he joined the group of gloomy-looking men.

'Well,' she heard Tony say. 'I think it's time we had a serious talk, Penfold.'

It was a relief when a flickering blue light outside the windows told them the police had arrived. Alex went out to speak to the officers and shortly afterwards Philippa had to leave the guests to show the doctor up to Lizzie's room.

By the time he had confirmed there was nothing seriously wrong with

Lizzie and Philippa had escorted him downstairs again, the police had left and the women guests were beginning to drift away to their rooms. Philippa was afraid that Alex's important evening had ended disastrously. Her heart ached for him. But all she wanted just then was to get home to the peace of the cottage. She searched for him to say good-night and found he had taken the men to his study. From outside it she could hear they were engaged in heated discussion.

Alex answered her knock and came out to speak to her, closing the door behind him.

'Philippa!' he said. 'Sorry I had to leave you to cope on your own. What did the doctor say?'

'Your mother will be all right. It's just a superficial cut with some bruising. But where are the police? They didn't stay long.'

'Gone to the farm. If the Laramys have any sense and tell them the truth, they could get off with a caution.'

'I see.' She studied his face, trying to judge his mood. 'So what about you? How are you going to deal with them?'

'I'm going to have to think about that very carefully. The Laramys have done more damage here tonight than I ever thought they could! The worst hasn't happened yet and I don't give up easily, Philippa. You should know that by now.'

'Yes.'

'I told you once,' he said, 'that there are two things important to me, things I'm determined to have. One is to make sure the estate is run the way I want it. The other . . . ' He gripped her arms. 'You must know by now, Philippa, what that other is! You do know, don't you?'

She nodded, unable to speak.

'Then you'll know I won't give up on that, either.' His voice softened as he saw she was shaken. 'You're looking worried, my darling. You mustn't ever be frightened of me! I'm angry tonight,

128

but not with you. You played like an angel.'

'Don't exaggerate, Alex! I did my best and now I've come to say good-night. The women have all gone to bed and your mother's settling down now.'

'Of course! You'll need help with your harp. And I haven't even paid you!'

'That doesn't matter. You're busy. I'll leave the harp and collect it tomorrow morning. You'll have more time then.'

'Yes. Do come tomorrow! Come whenever you want!' He drew her to him and kissed her tenderly. 'Good-night, my darling. Thank you for being here when I needed you.'

Martin was still up when she reached the cottage. He took one look at her.

'The Laramys?' he asked and she nodded, noticing his expression change when she told him Lizzie had been hurt.

'What the devil was Alex doing to

let her get involved?' he burst out.

'He tried to hold her back. But she's very headstrong.'

'I know.' Martin sighed. 'She's all right, though?'

'She will be.' Philippa could see he was concerned and wondered again how well he had known Lizzie in the old days.

'Dad,' she asked, 'did you ever hear if there was anything between her and Jeff Laramy all those years ago?'

'What made you ask that?'

'Just a feeling. He's so bitter and yesterday afternoon she let slip that she might have hurt him once.'

'The only time she had anything to do with the Laramys,' he said slowly, 'was after old Jacob Penfold gave her the sack and Jeff's mother took her in to help out at the farm.'

'So something could have happened when she was there!'

Martin frowned.

'She wasn't with them long. She ran off with Alex's father soon afterwards.'

'If he was his father! You heard what Jeff said.'

Martin's frown deepened.

'I can't believe that of Lizzie! I daresay Jeff was a bit sweet on her then. Most of us were. But he was older than the rest of us.'

'And harder hit, perhaps?'

'Could be. Whatever happened, he should have forgotten it by now. You have to let all that sort of thing go. You can't let the past ruin the present.'

'No.' Philippa moved to kiss her father good-night. 'I'm going up, Dad. It's been a heavy day.'

The following morning her father offered to go to the manor with her to carry her harp out to the van and looked disappointed when she said there were several men there who could help.

'I thought I might have asked after Lizzie,' he said and Philippa reproached herself for not realising that.

'Well, do come if you'd like to!'

'No. She won't want a lot of visitors.

I'll just pick her a few roses.'

Penfold Manor looked deceptively peaceful when Philippa parked on the forecourt that morning, only the cracked window being a reminder of what had happened the previous night. There was nobody about so she ran up the entrance steps and tugged on the heavy bell pull. After some time, Peggy Tucker opened the door and peered suspiciously out at her.

'Oh, it's you, Miss Southcott,' she said. 'What with the police and the doctor and all the comings and goings, I never know who's coming next.'

'I'm here to collect my harp,' Philippa explained, 'and to ask after Mrs Penfold. How is she today?'

'She's downstairs — would get up. I told her to stay put.' Peggy grumbled on as she led Philippa into the morning-room where Lizzie lay on the sofa.

'You're looking better,' Philippa said as she handed Lizzie the roses. 'Dad sent these from the garden and hopes you'll soon be quite well again.'

132

'I'm all right now,' Lizzie said. 'Such a fuss! Poor Peggy was left with all the breakfasts to see to!'

'Where is everybody?' Philippa asked.

'One pair have gone back to London — that miserable man, Tony, and his wife. The others are out with Alex, being taken round the estate.'

'So they didn't all leave?'

'No, thank goodness! Alex would have been impossible to live with if they had! I just hope they're impressed enough this morning to stay interested.'

Philippa looked more closely at Lizzie. She seemed better but she was still very pale, the cut on her face vivid against her pallor.

'So what happened after I left last night?' she asked. 'Are the police charging anybody?'

'Not yet. They came back here after they'd been to the farm and told Alex they'd have to make some enquiries in the village. I don't want to press charges.'

'Does Alex?'

'He'll be stupid if he does.' Lizzie gave a sigh and lay back, closing her eyes.

'Are you sure you're all right?' Philippa asked.

'Yes. I'm just regretting I made such a fool of myself last night.'

'What were you trying to do — reason with Jeff?'

'For one crazy moment I thought he might listen to me.'

'Yesterday,' Philippa began carefully, 'you almost told me something about Jeff. But then Peggy came in.' She waited but Lizzie did not respond. 'I got the idea you might have hurt him somehow when you were both young. Perhaps I was wrong about that.'

Lizzie sat up and swung her legs from the sofa.

'No, you weren't wrong. But talking of Peggy reminds me I haven't spoken to her yet about lunch. I've been ordered to rest today so she'll have to manage on her own.'

'Can I help?' Philippa volunteered. 'I'm not much of a cook but I could prepare the vegetables for her, if you like.'

'Oh, would you?' Lizzie smiled her relief. 'That's very good of you, Philippa.'

'I'll have to wait until Alex comes back to give me a hand with my harp so I may as well make myself useful.'

'Then let's tell Peggy. She'll be glad of some help.'

They were leaving the morning room together when the front door bell clanged. They looked at one another.

'I'll go,' Philippa said.

When Philippa opened the door she found Jeff Laramy standing there. He was wearing his suit and clutching a bunch of yellow dahlias.

He looked shamefaced and embarrassed when he saw her.

'Oh!' he said. 'I didn't think to find you here.'

'I came to ask after Mrs Penfold. I expect you have, too.'

'Yes — well — none of us wanted that to happen last night. Is Lizzie about?'

Lizzie had been hovering in the shadows of the hall but now she came to the door.

'I'm glad you've come. We can talk in the morning-room.' She turned to Philippa. 'Will you tell Peggy I'm having a rest and don't want to be disturbed?'

Philippa watched as Lizzie led the way to the morning-room with a downcast Jeff following her. Perhaps they can sort a few things out between them, she thought, if they're left on their own for long enough.

She was about to shut the heavy front door when her eye was caught by a movement near the entrance to the woods. Alex and his party were just emerging after their walk around the estate and were about to head towards the manor.

I must stop them, she thought in panic. If Alex bursts in on Lizzie and Jeff before they've had time to put things right, they may never have another chance as good as this!

9

Philippa ran out of the manor and down the grassy bank towards Alex and his party. He waved when he saw her coming.

'Philippa!' he said as she reached him. 'Of course — you've come for your harp! You're just in time for coffee before I move it into the van for you.'

'Peggy thought you might like coffee on the patio as it's such a lovely morning,' she improvised hastily.

The patio was on the opposite side of the house from the morning-room and could only be approached from within by way of the breakfast room. She saw Alex frown and held her breath.

Before he had time to object, Philippa said, 'If you'll take everybody round

138

there, Alex, I'll tell Peggy it's OK and organise enough chairs for you all. Right?'

She flashed a smile at the company and hurried back into the manor.

'On the patio?' Peggy grumbled when she told her. 'Does he think I've nothing better to do?'

'I'll carry everything out when you've made it. And I'll help you with lunch if you like. Mrs Penfold said you might be glad of somebody to do the vegetables.'

'Oh, she did, did she? Is she having coffee with them?'

'No. She's resting. She'll have hers later.'

I must keep them all away from Lizzie and Jeff, Philippa thought as she rushed to the breakfast room, reaching it just as Alex and the others appeared outside on the patio. The women had discovered Arthur Penfold's roses and were exclaiming over their beauty.

'They look happy enough,' Philippa observed when Alex stepped into the room to lift out a small table for the cups.

'So far. Tony's gone — couldn't get away fast enough this morning.'

'Your mother told me.'

'Is she coming out for coffee? She seems better today.'

'She'd rather have a quiet morning. I'll see she gets hers later. Can you manage here if I fetch it all from the kitchen?'

Alex regarded her quizzically.

'You're being very co-operative, too. What's up with everybody this morning?'

Guilt flushed Philippa's cheeks.

'Well, I'm here so I may as well make myself useful.' She hesitated, wondering how much he wanted to tell her. 'Was it very bad last night?'

'Bad enough. We were at it until the small hours.'

'But only Tony's pulled out?'

'The others are giving me time to work things out with the men. But I'm beginning to think I've taken on more than I bargained for.'

'That's not like you!'

'No. You've unsettled me, Philippa. I'm not sure of anything any more, least of all of you.'

'I'm sorry, Alex. It's just . . . ' But she could not explain. She shook her head and blurted out, 'I must go. I have to see to the coffee!'

She hurried away to the kitchen, troubled because her own doubts were making things worse for Alex. But it isn't easy for me, either, she thought.

When he looks at me like that I want to put my arms round him and tell him it's all right, that I do care. But then what? How much are either of us prepared to give up for each other?

Peggy had loaded a tea trolley with the coffee pot, a jug of cream, the cups and saucers and even a plate of biscuits. When Philippa returned to the patio, the smell of the coffee soon had everyone gathering round her. While she was pouring it, the woman called Jane, who had a cousin on the board of one of the London orchestras, lingered for a moment, wanting to know if Philippa had thought any more about being introduced to him.

The excitement of the previous night had driven the offer from Philippa's mind. Now she looked up with interest.

'I'd be delighted to have an introduction, if you could arrange it.'

'Richard will be with us next week-end,' Jane told her. 'He's coming for our daughter's twenty-first and we're having a lunch party for family and friends on the Saturday. I wondered if you'd like to play for us. You could meet Richard and he could hear for himself how good you are. He's with the Philharmonia and I'm sure he'd fix an audition for you.'

'Next week-end? I'm in Bristol on Wednesday and Thursday for the Arts Festival. It would be a bit of a scramble.'

'You'd stay with us, of course. We live in Surrey. I'll give you my card. Come up on Friday if you can manage.'

'It's very good of you.'

'Nonsense, my dear! Have a think about it! We're not leaving until tomorrow.'

'Thanks. I will.'

Jane moved away with her coffee, leaving Philippa in a state of exhilaration. The Philharmonia orchestra! Was it really possible? She saw Alex watching her. He came over to the trolley for his coffee and her hand shook as she poured it.

'You and Jane looked like you were up to something,' he said.

'Perhaps.' She explained about Jane's offer and saw his lips tighten.

'Well, there you are!' he said. 'I told you these people could be useful. Do you think you'll go?'

'I haven't decided. I've a busy week with the Bristol recitals.'

'But this is what you've always wanted, isn't it — a permanent job with an orchestra?'

'It's only an introduction, Alex! It's not even an audition yet!'

'Once he sees you and hears you play, that'll be it! You'll disappear, just as I've been afraid you would!'

'And if I don't disappear?' she challenged him. 'If I stay on in Penworth?'

'If you stay here in Penworth, my darling, we could discover what love is all about and why we were destined to meet one another again. This is where we belong, Philippa! We could set this place alight if we worked on it together!'

'You mean, you'd want me to give up my musical career?'

'No! You could always make music, give recitals. Why not? But I know what sort of lives orchestral musicians lead — always travelling — no time for their families. It wouldn't suit you, Philippa.'

'Let me be the judge of that!'

'Of course. It's your life!'

'Is it? Sometimes I think you've taken charge of it already!'

Their voices had raised and she

saw that some of Alex's friends were looking in their direction.

'You're neglecting your guests,' Philippa muttered.

'Just promise me you'll think this over seriously!'

'Don't worry! I intend to!'

When he left her she poured herself a cup of coffee and walked to the far side of the patio.

So that's the truth of it, she thought. I can have my music provided it doesn't interfere with what he wants of me!

I can entertain prettily for his friends or at the occasional concert but not take up a position in an orchestra! What sort of career is that?

Someone came up behind her just then and touched her elbow.

'Oh, aren't these roses wonderful!' Myrtle said in her ear. 'Did you ever see so many colours? And the perfume! This is such a beautiful house! So historic! Alex must be having a lot of fun restoring it.'

Restoring it, Philippa thought bitterly. Fun?

'Oh, this is nothing compared to the Valley Gardens,' she said. 'Has Alex taken you to see them yet?'

'He's mentioned them. A kind of obsession with his uncle, weren't they?'

'They were Arthur Penfold's life's work. But Alex talks of changing them, making them more formal.'

'I see.' Myrtle's eyes were probing. 'And you wouldn't like that?'

'Nobody in the village would. They're perfect the way they are.' Careful! Philippa thought. You're being disloyal to Alex. But her anger with him drove her on. 'Why don't you ask him to take you all down there now?' she suggested.

It had suddenly occurred to her that if Alex could be persuaded to take his party on a tour of the gardens, the admiration of people like Myrtle might make him see that they should be left unchanged. Not only that, he would be safely out of Lizzie's and Jeff's way for quite a while longer.

'I might just do that,' Myrtle said. 'I want to see everything there is to see before we leave tomorrow.'

She marched over to Alex, breaking in on the conversation he was having with her husband. Philippa saw Alex listen for a moment, then she heard him suggesting that they might all like to visit his uncle's Valley Gardens.

'Why don't you come with us, Philippa?' he asked. 'Or would you rather I loaded your harp for you before we go?'

'No. That can wait,' she said quickly, for above all she wanted to keep him out of the house. 'I've promised your mother I'll help Peggy with lunch.'

'That, too? You are being helpful today!' He turned to the others. 'Then shall we go? The walking's easier over grass, so I'll take you by the front way.'

'The back way's quicker!' Philippa intervened and saw a flicker of puzzlement in his eyes.

'But it's not so pleasant, is it?' he said.

He began leading his guests from the patio towards the front of the house. Once they had rounded it they would have to pass the morning-room windows where Philippa was afraid Lizzie and Jeff were sitting.

She could think of no way of preventing Alex from seeing them but trailed after his party in case there might be something she could do.

Just as they reached the forecourt and the manor entrance she saw, to her horror, that Jeff was standing on the top of the steps, evidently saying goodbye to somebody inside. At the same moment as Philippa caught sight of him, Alex looked up and saw him, too. He stood stock still for a moment. Then he bounded up the steps and seized Jeff by the shoulders.

'What are you doing here?' he snarled. 'Get out! Get out, Laramy!'

He gave Jeff a shove that sent him stumbling down the steps, half falling and ending up on his knees.

Philippa ran over to help him just as Lizzie attempted to push past Alex to assist Jeff, too. But Alex held her back.

'Leave him!' he stormed at Philippa. 'I suppose you're in on this! No wonder you were being so helpful today!'

'He came to apologise!' she cried.

'But not to you!' Jeff shouted at Alex. 'To your mother! Nobody wanted her to get hurt last night.'

'I know what your game is. You came to get round my mother! Well, you needn't try that again, Laramy! She's finished with you and so have I. So get out! Get out before I call the police again!'

Alex pushed his mother inside and slammed the door.

There was a moment's stunned silence. Then Jeff shrugged off Philippa's helping hand and rounded on her.

'He's a Penfold, right enough! I warned you, didn't I?' He swung round to Alex's astonished guests. 'And you lot had better watch out! He could turn on you yet!'

He brushed the dust from the knees of his best trousers, straightened his shoulders and began trudging away in the direction of the farm. Philippa watched him go with dismay. The guests, who had been shocked into silence, began to stir and mutter uneasily among themselves.

She knew she had to do something to save the situation.

'I'm sure Alex wouldn't want you to miss the Valley Gardens,' she said, 'so I'll take you down there, if you like. I expect he'll come along later.'

She smiled hopefully at them. Myrtle was the first to speak.

'Well, I'm all for seeing these gardens,' she announced. 'Whatever's going on here doesn't affect them. So let's go!'

Together, she and Philippa left the forecourt and began walking across the stretch of parkland that led to Arthur Penfold's hidden valley. The others soon followed. She was not looking after the guests for Alex's sake but for his mother's. Left alone with him, Lizzie might be able to explain why Jeff had called to see her that morning.

The gardens had several other visitors that Sunday and were looking particularly beautiful. The hydrangeas and fuchsias were in bloom and there were glowing banks of geraniums and pelargoniums, delphiniums, irises and lilies, swathes of coloured daisies and lavender and carpets of pansies under the trees.

Huge carp and goldfish flashed just under the surface of the largest lake and ducklings swam up to the little bridge, expecting to be fed. The visitors were very impressed.

'I can see what you mean, Philippa,' Myrtle said. 'It would be an act of vandalism to change any of this. It's so natural — the way I've always imagined an English garden should be. I shall tell Alex so.'

'Why does he want to change it?'

Jane asked. 'It's obviously popular.'

'People come from miles around,' Philippa said. 'But Alex has found a plan for an eighteenth-century garden he thinks would fit in better with his scheme for the estate.'

'Then he should lay it out somewhere else!' Myrtle said.

Philippa smiled to herself. She knew that the visitors would love the gardens the way they were and she hoped they would tell Alex this.

Just then, she remembered her promise to help with lunch and asked if the guests could find their own way back.

'Lunch is at one,' she said, 'but do stay as long as you like.'

She left them then and began hurrying towards the manor, seeing Alex heading towards her when she was halfway there. Her heart lurched at the sight of him. When they met he greeted her coolly.

'So what have you done with them, Philippa?' he asked.

'They're in the gardens. I thought it

better to take them out of your way for a while.'

'Did you? And what have you been saying to them — putting your case for leaving Uncle Arthur's gardens just the way they are?'

'No! That isn't the reason I took them there.'

'Really? You've done such a good job keeping me out of Jeff Laramy's way, why not out of the gardens as well? I didn't realise you could be so devious.'

She could not remember when she had felt so angry.

'Devious?' she flared up at him. 'I'd rather be that than so pig-headed I can't listen to anybody else's opinions! Everything I've done this morning was for your mother! First to give her a chance talk to Jeff who only came to say he was sorry, and then to give her time to talk to you! If that's being devious, I'm not ashamed of it!'

She tried to push past him but he caught at her arm.

'I'm sorry. It's been a bad morning.'

'Whose fault was that? Let me go! I said I'd help Peggy with lunch.'

'She says she can manage. So I've cleared the patio and loaded your harp into the van.' He handed her an envelope. 'This is for last night.'

She felt suddenly cold and nearly flung the envelope back at him.

'You want me to leave, don't you?'

'It's not that I don't want you! But I've a lot to do this afternoon. I have to persuade these people I can make a go of the estate without too much local opposition and I can't have any more distractions.'

'Or any different points of view?' she broke in. 'I understand, Alex! I understand perfectly!'

'No, you don't! You don't understand at all.' He caught her hands in his. 'You're the best thing that's ever happened to me, Philippa. But there are some decisions I have to take on my own. That doesn't mean I won't listen to your opinions, just that I can't

154

always agree with you. So don't think badly of me because of that! I'll ring you tomorrow. We'd better not meet until all this is over.'

'Oh, don't bother ringing! I'm going to be busy all week, perhaps for a lot longer than that. Goodbye, Alex.'

10

When Philippa reached the cottage, she opened Alex's envelope and found that he had paid her much more than she expected.

Strangely, that made her even angrier. What does he think he's doing, she raged. Paying me off? She was tempted to send his cheque back to him but then decided it would be more dignified to post him a formal receipt.

Doing that made her feel better and for the next few days she spent her time practising, knowing Alex would be involved with his guests until they departed on the Monday.

On Tuesday she left early for Exeter to rehearse with Sarah, stayed there overnight and drove with her to Bristol the next day for their first recital at the festival. One of the organisers put them up that night and their performance the next evening drew an even larger audience.

'You see? It's all happening!' Sarah said. 'And you're off to Surrey tomorrow! That invitation from Alex's friends is the chance of a lifetime. Won't you be too tired?'

'Yes, but I must go. It's their daughter's twenty-first and it's such an opportunity! A London orchestra!'

'Are you interested in the one being put together for next months' Plymouth festival?'

'Of course! I'm interested in anything that turns up!'

Sarah laughed.

'What's going on, Philippa? You're all keyed up these days. Is it because of that man — the one you said wasn't important?'

'No! He still isn't important!'

But even as she said that, Philippa knew that Alex had not only become important, he had disturbed her life completely. Apart from when she was playing and able to lose herself in her music, she thought about him all the time. She regretted their recent quarrel and kept wondering what he was doing and if he ever thought about her.

'Well, whatever it is, it's affecting your playing,' Sarah said.

'My playing?'

'It's much more passionate these days. I got quite carried away with you tonight. If you play like that you're bound to impress this man at the week-end.'

'You're imagining it!' Philippa said.

'No, I'm not. You were good before but now you're special. You must be in love, Philippa. I'm sure that's what it is.'

'Rubbish!'

But it was not rubbish, Philippa knew. She was in love with Alex, hopelessly in love despite her misgivings. But I can't give up everything I've worked so hard for, she thought, just because I happen to have fallen in love!

'Come on!' she said. 'I must get

home if I'm to drive to Surrey tomorrow. I'll drop you off at your place.'

It was very late when Philippa reached Penworth and her father was in bed. She let herself in with her key, glad that there would be no questions that night. But the next morning Martin was eager to hear how she had got on in Bristol.

She told him how well the recitals had gone and then asked, 'But what's been happening here? Have the police charged anybody?'

'Not yet. One of the village lads admitted throwing the stones that cracked the window and hit Lizzie, but he said he didn't mean to hurt anybody. Lizzie won't press charges so he could be let off with a caution.'

'So what about the Laramys?'

'That's all gone quiet because nobody knows what Alex is going to do. Jeff's as jumpy as a cat because he isn't sure if he'll really throw them out of the farm. It's beginning to look as if Alex is waiting for something to happen.'

'What sort of something?'

Martin shrugged.

'He might need to be certain how much money his business friends are putting up before he makes his next move. If he has to cut down on the changes he wants, he could think it better to leave the Laramys where they are, rather than break in a new manager.'

Philippa felt uneasy. Alex never did anything without a motive. So what was he waiting for?

'He rang on Tuesday and left a message for you,' Martin said.

Philippa's heart jerked.

'A message?'

'If you aren't going away this week-end, he'd like to see you tomorrow. Something important to discuss.'

'Did he say what it was?'

'No.'

'Well, I won't be here tomorrow so it'll have to wait.'

'He said it would be too late after Saturday.'

She felt a flush of irritation.

'Then why didn't he suggest today? I'm here until I set off this afternoon.'

'Because he said he was going away himself.'

He's doing this to make me choose between meeting him and going to Surrey, Philippa thought. What can he want to discuss with me that's more important than my chance to get into a London orchestra?

'Well, I'm sorry,' she said. 'I can't let these people down. It's their daughter's birthday tomorrow.'

All the same, when she was driving to Surrey that afternoon she could not help wondering if she was doing the right thing. Something important! What could it be? To do with the estate or to do with her?

The crazy idea flashed through her mind that he might have intended asking her to marry him but she rejected that immediately. They hadn't parted on friendly terms and Alex knew they'd have to sort things out first before she'd even consider it.

Still, it was an intriguing idea and as she cruised along the central lane of the motorway she found herself wondering what it might be like to be married to him. Not easy, that was certain. But might it not be rather wonderful, too?

Jane had given her directions to their family residence which proved to be a large, rambling farmhouse in the leafy countryside south of Dorking. Philippa immediately fell in love with the place, admiring its weathered brickwork glowing in the early evening sunshine.

She was warmly welcomed by Jane and her three daughters. There were two lively teenagers as well as Fiona, the girl at whose party she was to play. A marquee had been erected in the grounds for the guests as there would be a disco for the younger ones in the evening.

'A disco!' Philippa was dismayed. 'But I thought . . . '

'Don't worry!' Fiona said. 'We want you to play at the family luncheon earlier on. The disco will be much later. You're welcome to join us then, of course.'

This was not what Philippa had expected. She turned to Jane.

'Will your cousin be here?'

'He hopes to be at the lunch. Richard's a very busy man but I've told him all about you and he's looking forward to hearing you play. You must be tired after your long drive, Philippa. Fiona will show you to your room.'

What have I done, Philippa wondered as she followed Fiona up the twisting staircase. I've abandoned Alex for a girl who is obviously keener on her disco than hearing me play and the man I'm hoping to meet may not even get here! How you'll laugh, Alex, if he doesn't turn up!

'I'll need to move my harp from the van,' she said to Fiona. 'Where would be the best place to stow it?'

'Oh, we'll find somewhere. It must

be fun, travelling round with a harp!'

Philippa smiled. Everybody was showing her such friendliness she forgot her momentary disappointment.

'This is the first time I've played for a twenty-first,' she said. 'I'm really looking forward to it.'

From then on she became one of the family, revelling in the excitement of the preparations. She even ceased to care if Jane's cousin, Richard, came or not, so when he arrived just before they all assembled for the family lunch on Saturday, he was an added bonus.

The meal was laid out in the marquee which Fiona and her sisters had decorated with garlands of flowers. The guests sat on white chairs around white tables. Philippa was asked to play after the coffee was served

She was glad she had brought her favourite summer dress to wear, a full-skirted, lemon-coloured cotton one, and she was so relaxed by then her music flowed easily, rebounding from the canvas roof of the marquee. She had chosen light music, folk tunes and dances and some of her exciting Spanish pieces for which her audience demanded an encore.

She was flushed and happy afterwards and pleased when Richard congratulated her.

'Jane said you were good,' he said, 'but she didn't tell me how good! I'd be delighted to arrange an audition for you if you'll send me a copy of your cv. Here's my card, Philippa. We already have a regular harpist but there are occasions when we need more than one. So do get in touch! You'll probably be sent some music to try out with the orchestra. Have you had much orchestral experience?'

'Mostly at college or with local orchestras. But I've deputised once or twice. It's not easy to get a regular place when you play the harp. Sometimes I think I should have taken up the flute!'

He laughed.

'Well, don't give up! Keep trying!'

I will, she vowed. Whatever you say, Alex, I shall not give up!

Thinking about him made her wonder what it was he considered so important to discuss. Now that her part in the celebrations was over she could easily slip away and drive back to Penworth that afternoon, meeting his Saturday deadline. She was tired and would be late arriving, perhaps too late and he might not appreciate her coming even if she made the effort.

She felt she should go but it was almost five o'clock before she was able to get away. Jane and the girls were so sorry to see her leave. They paid her generously and she left with their good wishes ringing in her ears.

The thought of seeing Alex again set her pulses racing and she hoped he would be pleased that she was hurrying back for his sake. She drove fast, only stopping once for coffee in a service station and made good time until she left the motorway and the main roads and was into the last country stretch towards Penworth. Then everything seemed to conspire to slow her up.

When her speed dropped to ten miles an hour behind a tractor she was chafing with impatience. The narrow lane twisted and turned but she knew it well. It was usually quiet in the evenings so she took a chance and overtook where it widened for a few yards, just before a bend.

Too late, she saw the approaching car. She knew she had either to hit it or the hedge and instinctively wrenched the steering wheel hard over left, catching a glimpse of the horrified face of the other driver before she ploughed into the hedge, missing his car by inches.

The impact flung her sideways against the van door and she winced as her shoulder struck it. She heard the strings of her harp jangle behind her and an ominous crack as the instrument slid forward on its trolley and hit her seat.

The driver of the other car was already out of it and shouting at her.

She wound her window down.

'Sorry,' she said. 'I'm sorry.'

'What on earth were you doing, overtaking on a bend?'

'I was in a hurry. It was my fault.'

'You're lucky you're still alive! Are you OK?'

'Yes. A bit bruised. I'm more worried about my harp.'

'What?' He peered into her van. 'You've got a harp in there? What's happened to it?'

'I think I heard it break.'

The tractor driver had drawn up and climbed down from his cab.

'It's Miss Southcott, isn't it?' he said. 'I thought I recognised you.'

'Yes.' His face was familiar. A man from one of the local farms, she thought. 'I'm on my way to Penworth.'

'Well, you won't get any farther tonight. Made a good mess of your van, haven't you?'

Philippa opened her door and scrambled out, then gazed with a sinking heart at the crumpled wing and smashed headlight of her father's van. 'It's not mine. It's my dad's.'

'He's not going to be very pleased, then, is he?' the car driver said. 'Want me to ring him and tell him what's happened?'

'Oh, would you? I'll give you his phone number.' She reached into the van for her bag and scribbled on a used envelope. 'He won't be able to do anything without transport, so could you ring another number as well? It's for Mr Penfold at the manor. Ask him if he could come in his estate car and collect me and the harp. He's a friend,' she added as the man looked doubtful. 'I'll pay you for the phone calls.'

'No need for that! I'd better contact the police while I'm at it. And what about a garage?'

'I'll let the one in the village know. They'll send a breakdown lorry in the morning. Oh — what a stupid thing to happen!'

'You shouldn't have been in such a

hurry, should you? Well, if you're all right, I'll be off.'

'Yes. Sorry I gave you such a fright.'

'Just don't do it again!' He went back to his car and drove off.

The tractor driver turned to Philippa. 'Sure you're all right, Miss Southcott?' he asked. 'You look a bit pale. And it's a shame about your harp. I heard you play it in the church a few weeks ago.'

'I haven't dare look at it, but I'm sure I heard it crack.'

'Want me to get it out for you?'

'No. I'll wait for Mr Penfold. You must want to get home, so don't stay around on my account.'

When he had gone, Philippa climbed back into the van to wait for Alex. She ached all over and wanted to weep. She had broken her beloved harp and she couldn't remember ever feeling so bad in her whole life.

It was dark before Alex came and Philippa was half asleep, slumped in the driver's seat when he drew up ahead of her.

'Philippa!' he cried when he ran to the van and saw her. 'Are you hurt?'

'I'm all right.' She opened the van door and almost fell into his arms. 'Oh, Alex! Am I glad to see you!'

He held her close.

'What on earth are you doing here? Your father said you'd be in Surrey until tomorrow.'

'I got away early. You told me there was something important.'

'You came rushing back for me? Oh, my darling, nothing's more important than you! You could have been killed!'

'I was hurrying to hear your news. You said it was no good after Saturday. But, Alex — I think I've broken my harp.'

He cradled her to him.

'It can be mended. I'll take you home.'

She felt comforted in his arms and rested her head on his shoulder.

'I suppose it's too late now,' she whispered tiredly.

'Too late?' he seemed puzzled.

'For the important thing, whatever it was.'

'It wasn't as important as all that! Because you weren't around, I've had to put off the decision. But don't worry! We can discuss it another time.'

'What?' She drew back from him. 'You mean I've dashed home tonight and broken my harp because of something that isn't important after all? Oh, Alex, how could you?'

'Hush! Don't upset yourself! I must get you home. Your father's worried.'

She pushed him away.

'He'll be more worried when he sees his van! There's that, too!'

'We can send somebody out for it in the morning. Everything's going to be all right. Are you going to help me move your harp?'

She winced.

'No. You do it! I can't bear to see how badly it's damaged.'

Slowly, Alex opened the back of the van and peered inside.

'I'm afraid you're right,' he said. 'It

looks as if the top of the frame's broken.'

'Then be careful! Can you lift it without making it worse?'

'I'll try. Don't take it so badly! We'll get it to the best repairer we can find.'

'But what shall I do without it?' she cried. 'I play it every day!'

He came over to her then and wrapped his arms round her.

'You'll just have to make do with me, won't you? It might give us time to get to know one another better. Wasn't that what you wanted, my darling?'

What she read in his eyes then made her feel cold. Was that all it meant to him? Her harp was broken and all he could think about was that she would have more time to spend with him! She had hurried back from Surrey for nothing and he only saw her harp as something that had been keeping them apart, a nuisance that could easily be mended.

She turned away from him, choked

with disappointment.

'Just move it,' she said. 'I'll wait in your car.'

When he eventually climbed in beside her she could not bear to look at him. She hardly spoke a word on the way home.

11

Martin was so understanding about the damage to his van, Philippa felt worse than ever. He was more concerned about her and her harp.

'We can't do anything tomorrow as it's Sunday,' Alex said, 'but I could take it to Exeter on Monday if you know of a good man.' He glanced at Philippa. 'You could come with me.'

'I'll see,' she replied coldly.

He looked at her more keenly.

'You're all in. What you need is a warm bath and bed. So I'll go now and ring in the morning. You can tell me then what you want me to do.'

'Well!' Martin said when he and Philippa were alone. 'It's lucky Alex was available. But I'm sorry your week-end finished so badly. How was Surrey?'

'I must get to bed, Dad. I'll tell you all about it in the morning.'

How could she audition now without her harp, she asked herself. How could she give another recital with Sarah in a few weeks time or take part in the Plymouth festival orchestra?

If I hadn't come rushing back for Alex, she thought, none of this would have happened! And he doesn't care, that's obvious! All he thinks about is himself! My music is of secondary importance to him.

But Alex was on the phone soon after breakfast to enquire after her.

'I'm all right,' she said. 'And Dad's been on to the garage to move the van.'

'Good.' He hesitated. 'I need to talk to you, Philippa.'

'About something that's not really important? I'm not interested any more.'

'I must see you!' he said. 'If you're in church, I'll meet you there. But come to lunch. I'll tell Peggy to expect you and your father. Things have been happening here and I need to talk to you before I make a decision. And don't forget you're going to give me the name of somebody to repair your harp!'

He rang off, leaving her baffled. What was this thing that was unimportant one day and so important again the next?

'We're invited to the manor for lunch,' she told Martin, 'and Alex wants to know where to take the harp. I'd better ring Sarah. She'll know of somebody. And I'll have to tell her it may not be repaired in time for the Plymouth festival.'

'You'll need it for this audition as well, won't you?'

'If it ever comes off!' She had told him about Richard's offer over breakfast but an audition suddenly seemed an impossible dream and she sighed.

The news of her accident had travelled round the village and she and Martin were stopped several times on their way to church by people enquiring how she was. When they were within sight of the lynch gate she saw that

Jimmy was there, apparently waiting for her. He looked uncomfortable.

'Sorry to hear about the van,' he mumbled, 'and your harp. Are you OK?'

'Yes. It was my own fault, really.'

'Well, if there's anything I can do . . .'

'We'll manage. I've nothing much on for a while. But thanks, Jimmy.'

'I reckon Mr Penfold will see you're all right, anyway,' he said and Philippa could hear the bitterness in his voice. 'Not that we hear from him! We don't know if we're going or staying. Have you any idea what's going on?'

'Why should you think that? I've no idea what he's planning.'

'Well, if he lets anything slip we'd be grateful if you'd pass it on.'

'No!' She was sharp with him. 'I don't want to be involved! I've been in enough trouble already because of you!'

She would have pushed past him but he caught at her arm.

'For old times' sake, Pippa!' he pleaded. 'All we want is a quiet tip-off.'

'I told you before, you and your father must settle your quarrel with the Penfolds yourselves. You've only made it worse by stirring up the village and calling that ridiculous demonstration. I'm keeping out of it from now on!'

She hurried up the path and into the church porch where her father waited.

'What was all that about?' he asked.

'Just Jimmy expecting me to take sides again. But I've finished with all that.'

Martin looked back towards the lynch gate.

'He's stopping Alex now.'

Philippa watched, trying to judge from the young men's gestures whether they were quarrelling or not. She saw Alex shrug his shoulders dismissively and Jimmy march angrily away. Then Lizzie took Alex's arm and began gently propelling him towards the church porch.

When the service was over, Philippa was detained by several people concerned about her accident. Lizzie and Martin walked on while Alex waited, grinning when she eventually joined him.

'You're popular today,' he remarked.

'I'm a seven-day wonder, that's all.'

'Such exciting lives we lead in the country!' he mocked. 'Still, I'm pleased you're looking better and that you're coming to lunch. Have you an address for me for tomorrow, for your harp repair?'

'Yes. Sarah knows of a good man.'

'And you're coming with me?'

'I think I'd better. I want to know what he can do.'

'I'm sorry if I was insensitive about your harp yesterday,' he said. 'I didn't mean to be. I was worried about you. I'm not really jealous of it, Philippa. I know I could never fill that part of your life but there's all the rest of it, isn't there? That's why I must talk to you today. Will you come for a walk after lunch?'

She guessed what he was trying to do, to recapture the magic the hermitage held for them both. If it cast its spell over her again she knew she would be lost.

'If it's about the estate,' she said, 'don't forget there are other people involved as well as you!'

'I knew it!' he exploded. 'Jimmy Laramy was trying to get at me through you!'

'No! He and Jeff just want to know what their position is! Surely you could tell them instead of leaving them in suspense like this?'

'I'll tell them when I know myself!'

'I don't understand.'

'I can't decide anything, Philippa, until I know where I stand with you! You've turned my life upside down and I'm not certain of anything any more!'

'All right,' she said at last. 'If it means so much to you, I'll come.'

After lunch, when Alex suggested that he and Philippa should take a walk, they left Lizzie and Martin chatting in the sunshine out on the patio.

'Those two get on very well together,' Alex remarked as he and Philippa set off down the grassy bank towards the woods.

'I think my dad was one of your mother's admirers in the old days.'

'One of many, from what I've heard!' He sounded disapproving.

'She was very young,' she suggested. 'And, I believe, very beautiful.'

'Not too particular, either, to count Jeff Laramy among her conquests!'

'Did she tell you that?'

'After he came here last Sunday.'

'They quarrelled, didn't they, all those years ago?'

'That's why he's so bitter now. It seems he was kind to her then. When my grandfather kicked her out old Mrs Laramy gave her a job on the farm.'

'Dad did tell me that.'

'Then Mother discovered she was pregnant. She was too scared to tell her folks so Jeff offered to marry her to give the baby a name. Can you believe it? I might have been brought up a Laramy! Luckily for me my father did the honourable thing and ran off with her!'

If he was your father, Philippa thought.

'Jeff must have loved her very much to want to do that,' she said. 'Is this why you can't make up your mind about him?'

'Well, she knows she treated him badly. I don't particularly like the man but in a way I almost feel indebted. He's had a couple of nasty shocks lately and mother thinks he might be more co-operative now. But that's not the only reason I'm hesitating. The rest has to do with you, Philippa.'

He took her hand as they walked but did not speak again until they came to the hermitage. Then he led her inside it and said, 'I haven't asked you yet what happened in Surrey. What about the man who came to hear you play?'

'He was very kind. He asked me to

send him my cv and said he'd try to arrange an audition for me. But they already have a regular harpist so there's nothing definite.'

'I see.' Alex looked relieved. 'You've not signed up to anything, then?'

'Of course not! I knew that wasn't on the cards.'

'So what if you had another offer?'

'What sort of offer?'

He caught hold of her hands and began talking very excitedly.

'My backers were getting nervous last Sunday because of all the trouble with the locals and I must admit I was shocked when I saw how many villagers had signed the Laramys' petition. But just when it seemed everybody was going to pull out, Myrtle came up with an idea.'

'Myrtle?' Philippa was astonished.

'She's not as feather-brained as she looks! She's very taken with your music, you know, and she loves the manor. She suggested going easy on the changes to the estate and concentrating on the house instead — not just putting on eighteen-century banquets but opening it up for musical soirées as well. She and Lloyd were keen to back that and so were the others. We'd need a bigger music room, so they'd put up the money to knock the outer and inner halls into one. We could have musical week-ends when people come to stay. We're even marketing the United States. You could be in charge of all the music side! As well as giving your own recitals, you could invite all the best musicians.'

'You mean you're offering me a job?'

Disappointment made her heart plummet and she stared at him in dismay.

'Another way of life, Philippa! You'd have your music and we'd be together. I've been in London these last few days talking to an architect I know about the alterations to the manor. Myrtle and Lloyd are off to the States on Wednesday which is why I have to make a decision soon.'

She didn't know what to say. 'What about all your other plans — the sheep and the cattle?'

'I'll put all that on ice if you agree.'

'And if I don't?'

'They'll go ahead and if the Laramys make trouble I'll get rid of them.'

'That's blackmail, Alex! You could have your musical soirées and weekends without me!'

'No! They're for you, my darling! I know I'll have to give you something you want if I want you to stay here.' He pulled her towards him. 'And I want you so much, Philippa. I can't lose you now I've found you again. You belong here.'

She would have protested but his mouth closed on hers. Philippa clung to him and it was like the day in the manor library when she had known, without doubt, that all she really wanted was Alex. And yet there was still a small voice in her head that whispered, 'Take care! Not yet! Think about it! Think!'

When he let her go he asked, 'So what do you say?'

'It's too sudden,' she said. 'And I'd like to talk it over with my father.'

'There could be a place for him here, too — a workshop.'

'Don't try to buy me, Alex!'

'I'd never do that. I want you to come to me of your own free will. Out of love, my darling, because you just can't keep away!'

And that could so easily happen, she thought. But is this what I've been working for all these years — to bury myself away in the country, making music for travelling Americans and Alex's paying guests?

'I'll let you know,' she said. 'I can't decide something as big as this without thinking very carefully about it first.'

12

When Philippa told her father about Alex's offer, he said, 'This is something you must decide for yourself. There's more to it than just the music, isn't there?'

She lowered her eyes and could not answer. Martin sighed.

'I can tell that by watching you together. So how serious is he?'

'I'm not sure.'

'And you?'

'All I know is, I've never felt like this about anybody before. I imagine the music part of it would be strictly business and I'd be paid a salary.'

'It wouldn't be easy keeping that apart from whatever else he had in mind.'

'That's what worries me. The job could be interesting, even exciting. But I'm not sure if I'd be taking it on because of that or because I want to be with him. And if it didn't work out, where would that leave me?'

'More or less where you are now,' Martin suggested gently, 'only rather more experienced. But you're young and that's the time to take chances. All I can suggest is that you listen to your heart. It's usually a pretty good judge.'

'But Lizzie Ash did that!' Philippa objected. 'And look where it got her!'

'You're wrong! Lizzie took the easy way out when she ran off with John Penfold. If she'd listened to her heart she'd have stayed in Penworth and had her baby. She sees that now. She's sure Arthur would have defied old Jacob and married her once he saw his son. She'd have had the man she wanted and Alex would have been brought up by his real father.'

'Does he know that?'

'No. And she'll never tell him. He's a Penfold and that's all that matters to him. She only told me because we were good friends once.'

'Jeff Laramy offered to marry her. Did she tell you that as well?'

'Yes.' Martin smiled. 'Lizzie tugged a good few heart strings in those days.'

'Including yours?'

'Ah!' He chuckled. 'I was more cautious. You take after me there.'

So does he regret being cautious, Philippa wondered. Is he telling me not to be? Because if I listened to my heart, I know exactly what it will tell me!

She rang the instrument repairer early the next morning to make sure he could see them and then contacted Alex to tell him.

'I'll pick you up in twenty minutes,' he said. 'We'll find somewhere for lunch after we've delivered the harp and have a look round Exeter. There might be a show on at the theatre this evening. It'll be a day off for both of us.'

And time to get to know one another,

she wondered. A whole day in his company in which anything could happen? She felt apprehensive when he arrived to pick her up. There was admiration in his eyes when she opened the door to him.

'You look gorgeous,' he murmured. 'There's something about you, Philippa, something special. That's why I know you're so right for Penfold.'

She felt a flicker of unease.

'I'm not a commodity, Alex, like the antique furniture you're collecting!'

'No! You're flesh and blood and I adore you, my darling! But shall we go? I've wrapped your harp in blankets and packed it securely.'

'That was thoughtful.'

'It was Mother's idea,' he admitted and grinned.

Philippa laughed as she slid into the passenger seat of his Volvo and did not edge away when he climbed in beside her. She smiled up at him.

'I do like your mother.'

'And she likes you. The trouble is,

you both seem to have got my measure. So how am I going to keep any sort of authority with the two of you on my tail?'

'You don't know yet I'll still be around. We'd better go,' she whispered tremulously, 'or we'll be late for our appointment.'

'Plenty of time.' He kissed her gently before he switched on the ignition. 'We've all the rest of today and all tomorrow and the next day. There's nothing to take you away from me now so we can enjoy just being together.'

'Wait a minute!' she protested as the car moved off. 'I do have other things to keep me occupied! I have to prepare my cv for London, for a start.'

Alex's tone changed. 'You're going ahead with that?'

'Of course! I can't miss out on such a good chance.'

'But I thought — if you come in with me . . . '

'That won't be for ages. You said so. I can't just sit around waiting, even if

I accept your offer.'

'So you haven't decided yet?'

'I'm still considering it. And you said I could carry on with my own music until you were ready to start.'

'I wasn't thinking of London — more of your local work.'

'So what's the difference?'

'The difference, my darling, is that I've rather more in mind for us than just working together at the manor! You must have known that!'

Of course she had known that! She had known it from the look in his eyes that morning. She knew it now because of the way his words made her heart race. But she still did not know exactly what he intended.

If I refuse his job will I be refusing him, too, she wondered.

'London may not come off, anyway,' she said placatingly. 'It's difficult for a harpist to get a regular place in a professional orchestra. The best I could hope for would be a spot of deputising.'

She stole a glance at Alex and saw that his face had relaxed and that he was even smiling a little. He knows, she thought, that I'm unlikely to refuse him. So why do I pretend to myself that I actually have a choice?

When they reached the workshop, Philippa felt immediately at ease. From the gentle way the owner handled her harp, she knew she could trust him.

'You think you can mend it?' she asked warily.

'Oh, yes. I'm rather busy just now so it may take a while. Will you need a replacement? I can put you in touch with a very good hire firm if you want.'

For a moment Philippa was tempted but one look at Alex's face made her change her mind.

'No,' she said. 'I've nothing important until next month. Will it be ready?'

'In just a week or two. It's a lovely instrument, Miss Southcott, so I'm sure you won't want to be without it. I'll give you a ring as soon as it's ready.'

Alex took her arm when they were outside in the street again.

'Thanks, Philippa,' he said.

She smiled.

'Well, I didn't want to play any old harp. I'm used to mine.'

'Then I hope you'll become just as used to me,' he murmured in her ear, 'and never want a replacement.' That made Philippa blush and he chuckled. 'Now I've embarrassed you. What shall we do before lunch? It's early yet.'

'We could always have a look at the cathedral. It's ages since I was there.'

'And I've never been. You can show it to me.'

The Cathedral Close was full of people taking advantage of the sunshine, sitting or lying on the grass, reading or picnicking. Alex stared at the cathedral, its stonework almost golden under the bright light. 'It's very impressive.'

'Fourteenth century. Shall we go in?'

They entered by the main doorway. The sun was shining through the huge, circular, stained-glass window above it, staining the paving stones below with bands of colour. Alex took Philippa's hand and paused for a moment to stare at the soaring blue marble columns that supported the ribbed vault of the roof.

The atmosphere was hushed as they began walking round the building. Then someone began playing the organ and Philippa whispered, 'Let's sit and listen for a while.'

They found seats with a clear view of the altar and the tall windows behind it. When Alex slipped an arm round her she leaned against him, feeling a strong sense of belonging.

'I wonder who's playing? He's very good,' she whispered.

'Well, you're the expert! Actually, I was wondering something else — if it's very difficult to get married in here.'

'What?' She was so astonished the word burst out louder than she intended.

'I was imagining you, in a beautiful white dress, walking the length of this place. A bit daunting! I expect you'd prefer the village church.'

'What are you saying, Alex?'

'Just thinking aloud.' He smiled at her evident confusion.

'But — but you haven't even . . . '

'Hush!'

She stared at him wide-eyed, hardly believing what she had heard. So this was what he had in mind! Another way of life, he had said, but she had not realised that included being his wife!

She had idly dreamed of the possibility on her way to Surrey, but mistress of Penfold Manor? To settle down as Philippa Penfold, with all that entailed?

The organist was working up to a crescendo and her heart began racing with it. Alex would expect some sort of response once the music ended and what could she say to him? His arm tightened round her as the music crashed about them. Suddenly it all became too much and she jumped up, startling him.

'Sorry,' she muttered, and began

stumbling towards the exit.

Outside in the sunshine again, she took a deep breath to calm herself. Almost at once he was beside her.

'What is it?' he asked. 'What's the matter?'

He tried to put an arm round her shoulders but she jerked away from him.

'Did you have to do that — in there of all places?'

'Do what?' He seemed genuinely puzzled.

'Assume I would marry you! A job, you said, being together . . . '

'Well? Isn't that what marriage is all about?'

'I thought . . . ' She could not meet his eyes.

'What did you think, Philippa?'

'Oh, never mind! I didn't really know what you meant.'

He put his arms round her. 'Oh, my darling, I want you for keeps, not just for a fleeting affair. I know we could be happy together for the rest of our lives!'

'Don't! Oh, please don't!'

He drew away from her.

'What is it, Philippa? Did you really think I'd offer you less?'

'I didn't know,' she said. 'It's all been so sudden — first the music idea, then this! It's our whole lives you're talking about now, Alex!'

'Yes. So why don't we find somewhere quiet for lunch where we can discuss it calmly?'

They found an old pub off the High Street where they could get a bar lunch and he left her in a secluded corner seat with a table for two while he went to order. Philippa's mind was going over and over the same question. What could she say to Alex? To keep him waiting for a decision over a job was all very well but an offer of marriage was different.

She could walk out of a job if it didn't suit her. She could even walk out of an affair. But she knew she couldn't do that once she was married. So what was she going to say when he wanted an answer?

He came back with drinks for them both and when she took her glass she found that her hand was trembling.

'I've made you nervous,' he said. 'I'm sorry, Philippa. I shouldn't have blurted it out like that. But this has been in my mind for so long I somehow thought you knew. I've told you often enough how much you mean to me.'

She sipped her drink to steady herself.

'But marriage isn't something to rush into, Alex. It needs more thought than accepting the offer of a job!'

'Then take them one at a time!'

'But all these things are tangled up together, aren't they?'

'Not necessarily. I suppose you could work for me without marrying me.'

'That wouldn't be easy!'

'You could even marry me without working for me.'

'But you wouldn't like that!'

He sighed.

'Your work would take you away so

often. What I had in mind was more of a partnership, both of us together, making something of Penfold and the estate. You know the locals and I need you to tell me when I'm going wrong!'

'And love? Does love come into it at all?'

'Love!' She saw his eyes blaze. 'Love, my darling, would be the reason for it all! I love you so much none of the rest of it would matter if you weren't with me! I expect I'd go on working and planning and making money if you refuse me but it wouldn't mean a thing without you!'

He spoke with such passion she felt her heart swell in response. This, she realised, was what she had been waiting to hear, that she was more important to him than the Penfold estate.

So what could she offer him in return? Was he more important to her than her musical career?

Than her career, perhaps. She was not so sure about her music. But he was not expecting her to give that up, only to channel it in another direction, into another way of life.

So why am I hesitating, she wondered. How can I even think of refusing such a wonderful offer? Love and marriage with Alex and my music, too!

She laughed suddenly and saw his eyes open in astonishment and then fill with understanding.

'Philippa?'

She reached for his hand and held it tightly.

'I love you, too, Alex. I know that now. Success wouldn't mean much to me if you weren't around to share it. So I'm going to accept your offers — both of them, even though I don't suppose our life together will be all that easy!'

'Oh, my darling!' He moved closer to her on the corner seat, clasping her hands in his. 'What can I say?'

'Nothing!' She reached up to stroke his cheek. 'Don't let's stay in Exeter after lunch! Let's go back to Penfold. There's such a lot to talk about and so many things to settle. I'll forget about London and the cv so that we can spend as much time together as we need. But first I want to walk in the woods with you and I want you to take me to the hermitage and tell me all over again that you love me, because it's our special place!'

'And always will be! I won't move it, I promise, as it means so much to you.'

'Our very own folly! I'm coming to you the way you wanted, Alex, because I can't keep away any longer!'

'Philippa!'

He held her close then and kissed her with such passion she quite forgot where she was and kissed him back with a fervour that matched his own.

She was where she belonged, in Alex's arms, and would one day become what he so much wanted and she had only dreamed of being — mistress of Penfold Manor.

Other titles in the
Linford Romance Library

SAVAGE PARADISE
Sheila Belshaw

For four years, Diana Hamilton had dreamed of returning to Luangwa Valley in Zambia. Now she was back — and, after a close encounter with a rhino — was receiving a lecture from a tall, khaki-clad man on the dangers of going into the bush alone!

PAST BETRAYALS
Giulia Gray

As soon as Jon realized that Julia had fallen in love with him, he broke off their relationship and returned to work in the Middle East. When Jon's best friend, Danny, proposed a marriage of friendship, Julia accepted. Then Jon returned and Julia discovered her love for him remained unchanged.

PRETTY MAIDS ALL IN A ROW
Rose Meadows

The six beautiful daughters of George III of England dreamt of handsome princes coming to claim them, but the King always found some excuse to reject proposals of marriage. This is the story of what befell the Princesses as they began to seek lovers at their father's court, leaving behind rumours of secret marriages and illegitimate children.

THE GOLDEN GIRL
Paula Lindsay

Sarah had everything — wealth, social background, great beauty and magnetic charm. Her heart was ruled by love and compassion for the less fortunate in life. Yet, when one man's happiness was at stake, she failed him — and herself.

A DREAM OF HER OWN
Barbara Best
A stranger gently kisses Sarah Danbury at her Betrothal Ball. Little does she realise that she is to meet this mysterious man again in very different circumstances.

HOSTAGE OF LOVE
Nara Lake
From the moment pretty Emma Tregear, the only child of a Van Diemen's Land magnate, met Philip Despard, she was desperately in love. Unfortunately, handsome Philip was a convict on parole.

THE ROAD TO BENDOUR
Joyce Eaglestone
Mary Mackenzie had lived a sheltered life on the family farm in Scotland. When she took a job in the city she was soon in a romantic maze from which only she could find the way out.

NEW BEGINNINGS
Ann Jennings

On the plane to his new job in a hospital in Turkey, Felix asked Harriet to put their engagement on hold, as Philippe Krir, the Director of Bodrum hospital, refused to hire 'attached' people. But, without an engagement ring, what possible excuse did Harriet have for holding Philippe at bay?

THE CAPTAIN'S LADY
Rachelle Edwards

1820: When Lianne Vernon becomes governess at Elswick Manor, she finds her young pupil is given to strange imaginings and that her employer, Captain Gideon Lang, is the most enigmatic man she has ever encountered. Soon Lianne begins to fear for her pupil's safety.

THE VAUGHAN PRIDE
Margaret Miles

As the new owner of Southwood Manor, Laura Vaughan discovers that she's even more poverty stricken than before. She also finds that her neighbour, the handsome Marius Kerr, is a little too close for comfort.

HONEY-POT
Mira Stables

Lovely, well-born, well-dowered, Russet Ingram drew all men to her. Yet here she was, a prisoner of the one man immune to her graces — accused of frivolously tampering with his young ward's romance!

DREAM OF LOVE
Helen McCabe

When there is a break-in at the art gallery she runs, Jade can't believe that Corin Bossinney is a trickster, or that she'd fallen for the oldest trick in the book . . .

FOR LOVE OF OLIVER
Diney Delancey

When Oliver Scott buys her family home, Carly retains the stable block from which she runs her riding school. But she soon discovers Oliver is not an easy neighbour to have. Then Carly is presented with a new challenge, one she must face for love of Oliver.

THE SECRET OF MONKS' HOUSE
Rachelle Edwards

Soon after her arrival at Monks' House, Lilith had been told that it was haunted by a monk, and she had laughed. Of greater interest was their neighbour, the mysterious Fabian Delamaye. Was he truly as debauched as rumour told, and what was the truth about his wife's death?

THE SPANISH HOUSE
Nancy John

Lynn couldn't help falling in love with the arrogant Brett Sackville. But Brett refused to believe that she felt nothing for his half-brother, Rafael. Lynn knew that the cruel game Brett made her play to protect Rafael's heart could end only by breaking hers.

PROUD SURGEON
Lynne Collins

Calder Savage, the new Senior Surgical Officer at St. Antony's Hospital, had really lived up to his name, venting a savage irony on anyone who fell foul of him. But when he gave Staff Nurse Honor Portland a lift home, she was surprised to find what an interesting man he was.

A PARTNER FOR PENNY
Pamela Forest

Penny had grown up with Christopher Lloyd and saw in him the older brother she'd never had. She was dismayed when he was arrogantly confident that she should not trust her new business colleague, Gerald Hart. She opposed Chris by setting out to win Gerald as a partner both in love and business.

SURGEON ASHORE
Ann Jennings

Luke Roderick, the new Consultant Surgeon for Accident and Emergency, couldn't understand why Staff Nurse Naomi Selbourne refused to apply for the vacant post of Sister. Naomi wasn't about to tell him that she moonlighted as a waitress in order to support her small nephew, Toby.

A MOONLIGHT MEETING
Peggy Gaddis

Megan seemed to have fallen under handsome Tom Fallon's spell, and she was no longer sure if she would be happy as Larry's wife. It was only in the aftermath of a terrible tragedy that she realized the true meaning of love.

THE STARLIT GARDEN
Patricia Hemstock

When interior designer Tansy Donaghue accepted a commission to restore Beechwood Manor in Devon, she was relieved to leave London and its memories of her broken romance with architect Robert Jarvis. But her dream of a peaceful break was shattered not only by Robert's unexpected visit, but also by the manipulative charms of the manor's owner, James Buchanan.

THE BECKONING DAWN
Georgina Ferrand

For twenty-five years Caroline has lived the life of a recluse, believing she is ugly because of a facial scar. After a successful operation, the handsome Anton Tessler comes into her life. However, Caroline soon learns that the kind of love she yearns for may never be hers.

THE WAY OF THE HEART
Rebecca Marsh

It was the scandal of the season when world-famous actress Andrea Lawrence stalked out of a Broadway hit to go home again. But she hadn't jeopardized her career for nothing. The beautiful star was onstage for the play of her life — a drama of double-dealing romance starring her sister's fiancé.

VIENNA MASQUERADE
Lorna McKenzie

In Austria, Kristal Hastings meets Rodolfo von Steinberg, the young cousin of Baron Gustav von Steinberg, who had been her grandmother's lover many years ago. An instant attraction flares between them — but how can Kristal give her love to Rudi when he is already promised to another . . . ?

HIDDEN LOVE
Margaret McDonagh

Until his marriage, Matt had seemed like an older brother to Teresa. Now, five years later, Matt's wife has tragically died and Teresa feels she must go and comfort him. But how much longer can she hold on to the secret that has been hers for all these years?

A MOST UNUSUAL MARRIAGE
Barbara Best

Practically penniless, Dorcas Wareham meets Suzette, who tells her that she had rashly married a Captain Jack Bickley on the eve of his leaving for the Boer War. She suggests that Dorcas takes her place, saying that Jack didn't expect to survive the war anyway. With some misgivings, Dorcas finally agrees. But Jack does return . . .

A TOUCH OF TENDERNESS
Juliet Gray

Ben knew just how to charm, how to captivate a woman — though he could not win a heart that was already in another man's keeping. But Clare was desperately anxious to protect him from a pain she knew too well herself.

NEED FOR A NURSE
Lynne Collins

When Kelvin, a celebrated actor, regained consciousness after a car accident, he had lost his memory. He was shocked to learn that he was engaged to the beautiful actress Beth Hastings. His mind was troubled — and so was his heart when he became aware of the impact on his emotions of a pretty staff nurse . . .

WHISPER OF DOUBT
Rachel Croft

Fiona goes to Culvie Castle to value paintings for the owner, who is in America. After meeting Ewen McDermott, the heir to the castle, Fiona suspects that there is something suspicious going on. But little does she realise what heartache lies ahead of her . . .

MISTRESS AT THE HALL
Eileen Knowles

Sir Richard Thornton makes Gina welcome at the Hall, but his grandson, Zachary, calls her a fortune hunter. After Sir Richard's death, Gina finds taking over the role of Mistress at the Hall far from easy, and Zachary doesn't help — until he realises that he loves her.

PADLOCK YOUR HEART
Anne Saunders

Ignoring James Thornton's warning that it was cruel to give false hope, Faith set up a fund to send little Debby to Russia for treatment. Despite herself, Faith found she was falling in love with James. Perhaps she should have padlocked her heart against him.

AN UNEQUAL MATCH
Rachelle Edwards

Penniless and hungry, it seems that life could not be worse for Verena — until her father secures a marriage for her to the new Marquis of Strafford. Filled with disgust at this urchin, the Marquis leaves for France the day after the ceremony. But when he returns after two years, the situation is vastly different . . .

ASSIGNMENT IN VENICE
Georgina Ferrand

Freelance photographer Rhia Stacey was given the once-in-a-lifetime opportunity to collaborate on a book about Venice with the Marchesa di Stefano. But Rhia discovered an attraction to the Marchese Dario di Stefano, which could only lead to heartache.

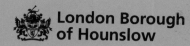